Rain

Book One
Der Drei Elemente

Guillermo Bosch

First edition published in 1995 as
A Richard Kazak Book
Masquerade Books, Inc.
New York, New York
ISBN: 1-56333-232-9

Second edition published in 2011 by
Fallen Bros. Press
ISBN: 0615551947

Third edition published in 2017 by
Fallen Bros. Press
ISBN: 0615551947

Fourth (Revised) edition in 2025 by
Fallen Bros. Press
ISBN: 0615551947

Kindle Edition published in 2016 by
Fallen Bros. Press

Kindle Edition (Revised) in 2025 by
Fallen Bros. Press

Cover Art: Hieronymus Bosch,
The Garden of earthly Delights, circa 1498
Cover design: © Guillermo Bosch, 2011
Chapter Illustrations: Hieronymus Bosch, ibid.

For Vincent,
and all those whose lives,
though masked,
make this story.

Author's Note:

For thirty years, Der Drei Elemente remained unfinished. When I finally returned to complete Fire, I realized the three books needed revision to create a more seamless connection. While each book stands alone, the revisions ensure they work together as true companions—siblings in voice, theme, and mythology.

These revisions were created with the assistance of Claude, an AI tool. Our collaborative process involved extensive dialogue about craft, consistency, and the mythic distance these stories require. I view this as an evolution of the editorial process, a new kind of partnership between human vision and machine capability.

Some readers will embrace this approach. Others will reject it. I'm comfortable with both responses. The work itself remains. What has changed is how that vision reached its final form.

I trust you will find the results of the complete trilogy worthy of the wait.

Guillermo Bosch

CONTENTS: PAGE

Prologue

Few know the final days of their lives with the certainty I know mine.

But that is jumping to the end of my tale while we are still at the beginning.

So, let us begin where my story begins, on the day hope died, on the 1,537th Day of the Drought when the hot southern winds turned the city's reservoirs into jagged crevasses of sun-baked clay and the streets into rivers of red eucalyptus leaves. Great billowing clouds of yellow dust blew in from the desert and turned the sun orange as it blazed in a green summer sky.

I was new to Central City then, an outlander, born and raised on the flatlands beyond the high mountains, on the lands where people made their living growing things, where it rained regularly, where people lived out the cycles of their lives marking the changes in the seasons, the heights of the trees and the births and deaths of their friends and neighbors. In those days, before I came to the city, I knew the names of every family within a day's walk of our village, knew their children and their trades and their histories.

But I had a great curiosity to know the world beyond the horizon, to see and smell and touch and feel things I had only seen in the picture paintings traveling merchants sold in our town during harvest festivals. I would fall asleep late at night dreaming about a different life in a city alongside the sea where the people came from across oceans and mountains and deserts to live together in one enormous potpourri.

And so one morning I left my village before the sun rose in the Eastern sky and I wandered west until my wanderings brought me to a place just like the one I had dreamed about; and once there, my world took on a shimmering vibrancy. There were people of all shapes and sizes and colors, speaking in tongues I had never heard, wearing garments woven from fabrics I had never touched. They dressed in exotic clothes, men looked like women, women looked like men, young children dressed like adults and many of the old people resembled children. The city vibrated with the echoes of hundreds of languages and thousands of accents, a babel that never ceased, not even in the deepest hours of night. Rich and poor alike ate bitter roots and sour berries and sweet herbs and fiery spices and the internal organs of animals, tiny fish from the deep seas, even little birds who never had a chance to fly. Food stalls lined every street corner, their vendors calling out in melodious chants that rose and fell like waves.

Each day my nose inhaled the city's perfumes, smoke from animal meat roasting over charcoal fires, sliced vegetables, pungent fruits, open sewers and sweating human flesh. The smells layered one upon another until the air itself seemed visible, thick with the traces of one hundred thousand lives being lived all at once. Each night I saw entertainments in the Central Plaza, dancing troops from the desert, storytellers from the hill country, mimics from the prairies and acrobats from the small villages along the southern coast.

But I was not really part of those things. I lived alone. I awakened each morning and looked at myself in the mirror. I bathed and shaved and put on my gray pants, my gray shirt and my gray jacket. I walked alone down city streets, through dangerous, exciting neighborhoods where people laughed and screamed, but I did not speak to anyone, and no one spoke to me. I would arrive at work and settle into my appointed place and pick up my writing instrument and take a piece of paper from my 'in' box and write on it, 'approved #329578,' and then I would move that piece of paper into my 'out' box. Day after day after day, the same motion, the same number, the same meaningless bureaucratic ritual.

At night I walked home through the same hot, animated streets filled with movement and scents and color and darkness and light, and each evening I returned to my small rented room where I ate cold food from tins and slept dreamless sleep on a narrow bed.

Then one day, after I had passed the vegetable market, but before I reached the man who wove baskets, I noticed a fortune teller had moved into what had been a vacant storefront in the second block on the left-hand side.

She was a lesser witch who had thick straight hair the color of burnt copper, big green eyes that saw through surfaces, and a large, long nose that gave her face a regal bearing. She sat on a purple satin couch near the doorway. When clients were present she dealt her tarot cards onto a glass-topped table with movements both practiced and mysterious. When they were not, she sat in a trance with her arms resting on her knees while she studied the cards and mumbled to herself in a language I did not understand.

One day, as I approached her storefront, I was walking more slowly than usual; and, as I passed by the fortune teller, I impulsively decided to go into the shop.

"I would like to have my fortune read," I told her.

She looked up at me, somewhat annoyed, and said, "You have been walking past me every day for two full moons and you have never even said hello."

I said, "I did not know you noticed."

Her eyes locked on mine. "And you would truly like your fortune read?"

"Yes."

She laughed, "You are lying."

I said: "No, I do not think so..."

"You would really like to sleep with me. That is what you would really like."

I stepped back and shook my head, but she only laughed again at my discomfort.

"Come back tonight," she said.

"Oh no," I said, "I could not..."

"Come back tonight," she said.

I did return that night, and when she took my hand, I followed her into the rear of her shop. There was a small room with a table, two straight-backed wooden chairs, an overstuffed easy chair, a single bed, a small refrigerator and one very old floor lamp that leaned at a precarious angle. The room smelled of incense and patchouli oil and something else I could not name, something both sweet and dangerous.

She told me to sit on one of the wooden chairs, then she took off her silver and purple shawl and tossed it onto the bed. Her flowered dress followed, then her thin black undergarment, then her silk under-clothing. She left her knee-length soft leather boots on.

She had the body of one who knows her own beauty, small breasts that tilted upward, a flat belly, abundant dark hair at her sex, rounded hips that tapered into long thighs, slender calves and narrow feet. My member, which had been without a woman for a long, long time, immediately stiffened. I stood up so that I could touch her, but she pushed me back down on the chair and ordered me to stay there.

Then she sat down in her easy chair and spread her legs over the arms so I was looking directly into the temple of her sex. She rubbed and kneaded her breasts while she slid her tongue across her lips. She pinched her extended nipples, and then licked her fingers until they were soaked with her saliva. Then she very gently put one finger onto the pearl of her pleasure and softly pleasured herself with one hand while the other continued to work her left breast.

I worshipped her. My eyes adored each part of her body, the folds of her skin, the thin sheen of her sweat, her rippling muscles, her toes, her ankles, her calves, her knees, her thighs, her buttocks and her navel, her long slim back, her shoulders and her breasts, her breasts with their swollen peaks, her neck, her chin, her lips and the dimples at the corner of her mouth, her nostrils, her nose and her cheekbones and her ears and, yes, her earlobes and her brows and her thick, soft copper hair...

I trembled and released with such force my body raised up off the chair and my seed shot onto the floor two meters away from where I sat holding my rigid member in my cramped, vibrating hand.

I could not leave her after that experience, not that night, nor the next night nor for many nights after that. In fact, I might never have left if the terror had not descended on Central City.

I suppose I should have seen the trouble coming, but I, who liked so much to watch, simply did not see the signs that were apparently obvious to almost everyone else. We all knew commerce had slowed to a trickle and jobs were scarce. There were official decrees when large investment houses went bust, banks were failing and the financial markets had collapsed. More and more tax revenues went to propping up the city's faltering institutions rather than improving people's lives. And then, while anger and resentment festered in the streets, the Central Authorities proclaimed laws that stripped the resisting classes of even the meager relief given during the good years. Droves of poor, homeless people were living in parks and along the walkways. The extreme heat and lack of water put everyone on edge. Murders, rapes and thefts became commonplace. There were fire bombings. There were assassinations. The city was a powder keg waiting for a spark.

Even so, I was lulled into complacency by my daily routine, and I have to say the 1,537th Day of the Drought did not seem different than any other day. As usual the sun rose into a cloudless sky. That morning, when we made love, my fortune teller complained the hot, dry weather made her burn. Her forehead broke out in a sweat but the droplets dried before they reached the end of her nose. She constantly flicked her tongue across her full, arched lips to keep them cool and moist. When she reached her climax, her body turned crimson from her breasts to her thighs, a flush that spread like wine.

I remember how intently I watched her as she walked away from our bed. I was still very much aroused by her, particularly by the sway of her hips and her thick copper hair whipping in the fierce dry wind that blew through our open window...

I am certain I was still watching her naked form when I heard the womp...womp...womp from the rotors whirling atop flying gunships in the distance. Their faintly menacing din floated on the edge of my consciousness until the racket grew so loud I could not help but realize the machines were hovering in the sky right above our heads.

I believe it was at that point when an amplified voice announced: "Those members of the resisting classes presently occupying Storefront #716, Attention! Attention! You have exactly fifteen seconds to vacate the premises before this location is extinguished. Attention, Attention..."

We were #716. I leapt from the bed and ran toward my lover. She whirled around and stared into my eyes. Her face was contorted by alarm and fear. She held her right hand out toward me, the tips of her fingers almost touched my face when everything exploded in a huge fireball.

The Central Authorities did not even give us the full fifteen seconds...

When I returned to consciousness, I was coughing, and I had a great deal of trouble breathing. The air around me was filled with the sweet rotten smell of sulfur and the acrid scent of burning wood. I remember I was in total darkness. I slowly and very carefully tried to move my fingers and toes, then my hands and feet, then my arms and legs. I was relieved to find everything worked.

However, as I tried to move about, I gradually realized I was in a pocket created by the debris which had piled up around me when the storefront collapsed from the force of the explosion. For a while, I felt better, or at least, hopeful, then I panicked when the overwhelming awareness that I was buried alive reduced me to a whimpering, frightened animal. I slithered and skittered about, trying to find an escape. The darkness was absolute. The weight of the rubble pressed down from all sides. I could feel the walls of my tomb closing in.

Then I touched something soft, cool and moist. At first I was curious, then I recoiled in horror. But I forced myself to touch again, forced myself to accept what I desperately wanted to deny: That flesh was familiar to me, the hair, the eyes and cheeks, the nose and mouth and chin of the woman who had, only moments before, given meaning to my life.

Then...

Then, my hands moved from her chin to...

To nothing. Her head was no longer attached to her body. I screamed, the noise reverberated through my burial chamber and the effort burned my throat. Then I scampered away from that spot as quickly as I could.

In the darkness, my head hit a supporting beam. Pain and

fear coursed through my veins, and I vomited uncontrollably. My stomach and chest muscles ached, and my head spun in increasingly dizzy circles. As I lay there in the debris and filth, inhaling the stench from my own vomit, I began to consider how long I could survive in my tomb. The air was growing thicker. The heat was becoming unbearable. Then I heard whispering noises off to my right.

I crawled in the direction of the whispers, and, as I approached their source, I realized they were not whispers at all, but normal voices muffled by a wall. I placed my ear against the mortared stones to try and hear what the voices were saying, but they were speaking a language I could not understand.

I sat with my back slumped against the wall and tried to decide what to do. I was certain if I began tapping on the stones they would hear me, but I could not make up my mind if I wanted them to hear me. After all they did speak an unfamiliar language, so I knew they were certainly outlanders, and therefore probably members of the resisting classes. But not necessarily. Many outlanders worked for the Central Authorities to secure their right to remain in the city.

On the other hand, what did I have to lose? If they were outlanders who worked for the authorities, I would probably only face summary execution.

That was preferable to being buried alive, so I tapped.

Rain

Chapter One: Meaning

Life has meaning.

Of course, there are no gods, no heaven, no hell. The old nations are finished; politics, totally corrupted. Money has no value. There is no compassion because we do not care about one another. But there is always the living itself. Life is meaning; it is death that is meaningless.

And I chose to escape death. I chose life when I was pulled from beneath the rubble by the members of a militant cell of the resisting classes. Of course it could also be said they were the same people who almost killed me because the explosions from the Central Authorities' flying machines were clearly meant for their storefront, not the lesser witch fortune teller's.

The leader of the cell was named Maria. Her mother, father, two sisters and three brothers had all been killed in a raid on their small coastal village. Maria had been away at the time, visiting relatives in the northern provinces, learning traditional healing arts from an aunt who knew the old ways. When she returned she found all traces of her home and family had simply vanished, bombed, burned, bulldozed and buried. The beach where she had played as a child was cratered. The house where she had learned to cook and sew and sing was nothing but ash. When she went to the Central Hall of Records, there was no evidence her family had ever existed.

In one sense, the thoroughness of the authorities worked out well for Maria, since it meant she did not exist either. She was thus invisible, a ghost walking among the living, and therefore free to do whatever she wanted.

And she knew what she wanted to do, kill everyone who had anything to do with killing her family.

But that was not so easily done. Meanwhile Maria waited. She found work as a hostess in a cafe where the rich and powerful mixed with the underclasses. She listened. She watched. She remembered. She learned a great deal because, on the surface she was the perfect, pretty, compliant, smiling servant. People told secrets and passed on dangerous gossip in her presence. They discussed plans and strategies Maria should never have heard. They targeted people and named names. She served them wine and cleared their plates and all the while she catalogued their crimes, storing each confession away for future reckoning.

Eventually she was recruited by the underground. In time, she became one of its leaders.

After she and her comrades pulled me from my grave, I collapsed yet again, so they wrapped my unconscious body in heavy woven blankets and carried me off to a safe place. I do not know how long I was unconscious. Time had become meaningless to me. When I finally came back to myself, I was lying on a narrow bed in a small, hot room. The walls were bare plaster, cracked and stained with water damage from years past when rain still fell. A single window, its glass long ago broken and replaced with oiled paper, let in diffused sunlight that turned everything the color of old honey.

When I awakened fully, Maria was standing in front of me in a white linen nightgown that smelled faintly of patchouli. I could see the shadow of her form through the thin fabric, her dark nipples and the abundant curls at her sex visible when she stood in the sunlight that streamed through the half-open window.

Her wide brown eyes questioned me. A single strand of hair

hung across her left cheek and stuck to the moisture on her upper lip. She folded her arms under her breasts which only exaggerated how round and full they were.

She smiled. "You are lucky to be alive."

"Am I?" I said. "Why?"

"Perhaps...perhaps you were meant to live, to..." she was very cautious, as if testing whether I could be trusted with dangerous knowledge.

I spoke slowly, carefully, my own anger and despair slowly bubbling toward the surface: "I have nothing to live for."

"You may have a great deal to live for," said Maria. She looked at me carefully, studying my face as if reading a map only she could see, then she continued, "There are those of us who would make the Central Authorities pay for what they have done to you...and others."

I believe I merely nodded and then said, "Well that may be, and I wish you luck, but that has nothing to do with me."

Maria shook her head and left me on the bed. I watched her through the unclosed door while she went to get a basin and a pitcher of warm water. I saw her nightgown stretch tightly over her rounded hips when she leaned over to splash water in the basin. I saw the taut muscles in her legs as she stretched to reach a high shelf. I watched the hem of her gown ride up to reveal the soft curves of her thighs when she reached for a large aquamarine towel which she brought into the room and dropped on the floor next to my chair.

I was actually surprised when I felt my member stir, and then harden so soon after losing my fortune teller. The body has its own wisdom, its own insistence on continuing despite grief. Maria smiled when she saw the evidence of my arousal beneath the thin blanket. "Take off your clothes," she said.

While I undressed, she poured scented oils into the basin. The smell of citron and rosemary filled the room, cutting through the oppressive heat and the stale odor of the city.

"How do you have water when no one else does?" I asked her.

"I know the people I need to know to have what I need to have," she said.

I was confused. "Then whose side are you on?"

"More importantly," she said, "whose side are you on?"

I ignored her for a moment and eased myself onto a bench near her bed. When I was comfortably settled against the hard wood, I dangled my arms over the edge of my seat. My left hand touched a bench leg. My right hand brushed against Maria's thigh, warm and alive. "I have never been on anyone's side," I said.

Maria reached for a soft white cloth and began to wash my body. She ran the cloth between my toes, slowly, one toe at a time, with the patience of one performing a sacred ritual. She nestled my leg under her arm and gently rubbed the soles of my feet. She lifted my foot and braced it between her breasts so she could easily wash along my calves and up my thighs. My toes wiggled against her flesh. The water streamed across her breasts, and dripped, drop by drop into the basin from the tips of her nipples.

Maria held my stones in her right hand and washed the skin at the top of my legs and around my member. At that point, I had a full erection, but she gave it no notice, treating my arousal with the same calm attention she gave to washing my feet.

She made me lean forward with my hands on the floor while she washed my buttocks. She draped a corner of the cloth over her index finger and slowly, gently turned her finger in slow circles within me, a strange intimacy that should have embarrassed me but somehow did not.

Then Maria set that cloth aside and started on my back with

another. "Now, sit back down," she said softly as she washed my stomach, my navel, my chest. She carefully sponged the burns on my arms, the scorched flesh from the explosion that had killed my fortune teller. I believe that was when I groaned. "The pain will not last," she said. I groaned one more time. Her eyes fluttered. She was embarrassed. "I am sorry," she said, "but we need to clean you. It is important. Your wounds are filthy."

After Maria washed my body and my face, she scrubbed my hair and massaged my scalp. I remember I actually dozed off while her fingers pressed against my neck, releasing tensions I did not know I carried. Then, when I opened my eyes, she stood in front of me, spread her legs and brought my head against her belly while her thumbs kneaded my shoulders. She was very strong. "I could snap your spine right here," she murmured as she stroked the bones at the base of my skull.

I tried to raise my head, but I could not. "Why would you do that?"

"I did not say I would...I said I could."

"Then you are trying to frighten me?"

"No, I only want you to know I am not your enemy."

Then she helped me stand up, and she wrapped the aquamarine towel around my body. She took my hand and led me into an empty room. She spread other towels and a few pillows on the floor. The heat was already oppressive, making the air shimmer and dance. "Lie down," she said.

While I settled myself onto the floor, Maria produced a soothing ointment which she rubbed into the burns on my arms. The salve was cool and smelled of aloe and something medicinal I could not identify.

"What is your name?" she asked, "And where do you come from?"

I was afraid to tell her. When I did not answer, she deliberately rubbed harder than she needed to. Another reminder of the balance of power between us. I cringed. "I would like some answers," she said.

So I began by telling her, "My name is Sandro, and I am an outlander." And then I told her how I came to be in the bombed-out storefront. I told her about my gray clothes and my meaningless work. I told her about the fortune teller and how she had made me feel alive for the first time in my life. I told her about the fifteen seconds we did not have.

She listened and asked questions. I answered them when I could. Sometimes she asked me about things, political and economic things, with which I was unfamiliar. Sometimes she explained what her questions meant, but she avoided any information which would reveal anything about the organizational structure of the underground.

When she was finished, Maria said: "So, Sandro, you are now alone and you have no one. You are a handsome young man, but other than that, you possess few talents or abilities or strengths..."

"I guess...yes, I guess that is true," I said. I was embarrassed, and I hung my head against my chest.

Maria lifted my head with her hands. She looked directly into my eyes. "No, that is not true. But to use your abilities, you must know your fear and your anger. Do not let them defeat you. Instead, learn everything, watch and listen, and you can give a great deal back to us...and to the people, to the people who suffer so much...even more than you have suffered."

Then Maria stood up and pulled her wet nightgown over her head. I gasped when I actually saw her skin, it was flawless, smooth, the color of milk and chocolate. Her breasts, despite their size, hung beautifully, supported by her wide shoulders and broad back. Her stomach was long and bulged, just slightly, above the dark curls at her sex. Her buttocks were round and full, but her hips were slim and tapered into long, well-muscled legs. She was magnificent.

Maria smiled. "Do not touch me. You are really not ready for that."

She hovered over me for a few seconds. I tried to speak again, but she pressed her finger against my lips and shook her head. Then she lowered her face to my member, and her masses of black curls covered my groin as she took me inside her mouth.

She did not begin her work right away. She merely kissed and nuzzled my flesh, her tongue moving along my length and circling the crown. She was not in any hurry. She moved slowly, ever so slowly, humming and moaning as she went, kissing and licking and licking and kissing...

I tried not to move at first. I wanted to just lie there and let the alternating sensations of pleasure and pain ripple up and down my body; but my stomach began to quiver and tighten and the muscles in my buttocks tensed.

Then Maria's lips tightened around me and she began a measured rhythm, increasing the pace ever so gradually, but moving faster and faster, taking me deeper and deeper into her mouth with each movement. Her curls brushed against my thighs and my lower stomach. I watched the twin curves of her hips flow up and down behind her curls. Her soft sounds escalated into extended groans.

Beads of sweat appeared on her back and buttocks. As the pace grew more furious her sweat formed rivulets which moved into the valleys along her spine, and still her lips grew tighter, the pace quicker, and the curls lashed across my groin, her brown skin pumped up and down, her lips and her curls and her movements, and her lips and her curls and her movements, and her lips and her curls...

I could not wait any longer although I wanted her to go on

like that forever. My release started deep within and traveled quickly along my length, only to hesitate for a moment before I spent my seed into Maria's mouth. She responded in a frenzy of motion and intense sounds, and her hair whipped across my stomach leaving red marks.

My head was pounding as her mouth left me. When I looked up and saw her face, I was transfixed watching my seed on her lips and chin. Her eyes were unfocused, her lids half closed, her nostrils flared, her breathing rough, uncontrolled, uneven. She groaned and stuck out her tongue to capture the last white pearl at my tip. Then she opened her mouth again and took the entire length of me in with one long, slow inhalation, and I fell backwards onto the pillows.

Sometime later, I awoke to a loud rumbling noise. I tried to shake the dizziness away, and figure out where the noise was coming from. It seemed familiar to me and I involuntarily mumbled, "Thunder..." Then, realizing what I had said, I became excited and shouted, "Thunder, that is thunder!"

Maria hushed me. "Be quiet, you fool. Do you want them to hear you?"

"Who?"

"That is not thunder. That is the sound of the heavy wagons passing on the street. The Central Authorities are moving bodies from the old camps to the new ones on the other side of Central City."

"I am sorry. I thought it might mean the rain had come. I thought...maybe..."

"There will be no rain," she said. "The bulletins say this is the 1,539th Day of the Drought. It will not rain today, nor will it rain for a very long time, not until this evil has been removed from the land and the people are free."

The muffled shouts and occasional screams which accompanied the sounds of the rumbling wagons confirmed Maria's description of their source, and the hot air blowing around the room from the ceiling fan confirmed her predictions of another hot, dry day. I closed my eyes and tried to remember the sound of real thunder, the tapping of rain on the roof, the sound of raindrops striking pools of rainwater, the smell of moisture in the air, humidity. My memories were fading like photographs left too long in the sun.

"Maria," I said, "Maria, tell me what it is like when it rains."

Maria sighed. She sat down beside me and stared at the ceiling as if she could see through it to the cloudless sky beyond. "It is like the world having one terrific climax," she said. "Everything is wet and smooth and soft, and the earth shakes and white lights flash in the sky and the air gets so heavy we can hardly breathe, and the water rustles the leaves of the trees and rushes down the hillsides and washes across the streets and, and...and then, when it stops, everything is calm, and everything is peaceful, and we are satisfied."

I felt Maria's words as much as I heard them. They calmed me, and a certain resolve settled over me like a blanket.

"I will help you," I said, "But what can I do?"

"You can work where I work," Maria said. "All kinds of people go there. They will like you. You will be invited to...They will want, want to...Things will...anyway, you will understand better after you have been there awhile."

I said, "I do not know how to be a spy."

Maria laughed. "It is not difficult," she said. "You just need to do what you are told and have a strong desire to please people. You will be fine. Trust me."

"But what will I do?"

"I already told you: watch...watch and listen."

"And what will I do with what I see and hear?"

"We will talk about that another time. Rest now."

Maria stretched her arms up toward the ceiling, then she

lifted her already-dry, wrinkled nightgown off the floor and pulled it over her head. I turned over onto the pillows. The heat had made me very tired. My lids grew heavy, and I immediately fell asleep, dreaming of rain falling on a city that had forgotten what rain looked like, dreaming of my fortune teller alive and laughing, dreaming of a world where hope had not yet died.

Rain

Chapter Two: Power

Power is a dangerous drug.

The most humble person can live a life of total deprivation, but if sudden good fortune brings that person power over another, the humble one suddenly wields an iron fist and revels in a sense of omnipotence.

Then power rushes through the veins and enters the brain. The powerful person demands special treatment, special considerations, special goods and services. What is more, they get them. Next, their power eats away at the heart. Lovers are cast aside. Friends thrown over. Family denied. When power reaches the spirit, total corruption sets in. The powerful person's humanity is extinguished, smothered by the utter certainty that one exists beyond the parameters set for mere mortals.

My new life required me to become an expert in recognizing and dealing with power. I worked at the Number One Cafe Bar & Grill for one hundred and fifty-four days before the Director of Finance noticed me. During those days I learned to read the subtle hierarchies of the powerful. I never spoke unless I was spoken to. I never indicated the slightest interest in the conversations of the patrons. I accepted abuse and praise with equal aplomb. I observed seductions, takeovers and blackmail, and I never batted an eye.

The cafe was a dimly-lit converted warehouse on the roughest edge of the Red Zone, where respectable people would not normally venture but where power brokers came precisely because it was dangerous. The tables were jammed right next to each other, coarse butcher's paper substituted for tablecloths, the floor was unvarnished wood and the noise was often deafening. The food was good, different enough to be adventurous, but never so different that it would upset a Director General's palate. But there was no denying the Number One's success as a meeting place for all the elements of Central City. Crowds gathered in front waiting to get in. The wine flowed, the drugs were plentiful, the pretty young girls and boys lounged about waiting to be asked.

And Maria managed the whole affair. She chose what people sat at which tables, the powerful along the outside of the room where they could see and be seen, the beautiful on the inside where they served as decoration, the scoundrels sprinkled among both where they could facilitate necessary transactions. She made introductions; she quieted disputes; she smoothed the way for commerce and diplomacy. She was everywhere and she was nowhere, for, despite her attractiveness, she maneuvered to keep everyone's attention on the patrons themselves.

On an uncomfortably hot evening on the 1,691st Day of the Drought, Maria slipped behind me while I was trying to cross the crowded room with three plates precariously balanced on each of my arms. She whispered in my ear: "There is a woman, a very powerful woman, who wants to speak to you. You must go to her."

As my eyes swept the room, I picked up the subtle signals from a woman sitting alone in a far corner of the cafe. She wore dark glasses, a black single-breasted suit, a white silk, mandarin-collared blouse, opaque white stockings and black leather three inch heels. Despite her formal clothes, she sat comfortably among the low-life on a simple, wooden, straight-backed chair. She held a cigarette in her right hand,

and a portable communicator in her left.

When I approached her table, I noticed her face framed by sleek auburn hair cut fashionably short. She had high cheekbones, a faint brush of hair across her upper lip and long, narrow fingers, the tips beautifully manicured. She was of medium build: her breasts not large enough to break the line of her suit, her shoulders narrow enough to use her jacket's subtle shoulder pads to advantage. Her hips were wide, but not large; her legs short, but not stubby. She had little ankles and pretty feet.

I stood in front of her as Maria had instructed me to do waiting for her to address me, but she did not smile, speak or laugh. For some time she leaned forward in her chair, her elbows on the table, her chin resting on her folded hands. She appeared to be staring intently at me, although for all I could tell, she may have been sleeping behind her glasses. I remained silent, counting my breaths to keep myself calm.

Finally she spoke: "Do you know who I am?"

I told her the truth: "No."

"I am the Central Director of Finance." I did not react, although my heart beat a little faster. She seemed surprised by my apparent lack of reaction, but also pleased. She almost smiled. "That means nothing to you?"

"It means you are very important."

"Yes, you are right. I am very important. Come." She held out her hand.

I panicked for a second because I did not know whether I should touch her or not. Then the woman solved my problem by taking my hand in hers and leading me out of the Number One. "I am to be addressed as Madame Director," was all she said.

As it turned out, The Director of Finance had a two-story apartment in the Central Governor's Building. Two walls were gray, smoked glass from floor to ceiling. When I looked through the windows I was able to see the lights of the entire city spread out like a carpet of stars, and the darkened mountains beyond. Off to my right I saw a sliver of the sea as the rising moon shimmered across the water.

One of the other walls was covered with long swaths of rich fabric in deep burgundy and gold. There was a decorative hand-woven carpet on the floor, but the furniture was simple, straightforward. Under the circular stairway to the second floor, there was a small alcove filled with computational equipment and electronic picture screens that glowed with constantly shifting numbers. There was a massive tapestry hanging on the far wall which was, as I realized when I stared at it more closely, a surreal depiction of a woman's sex.

When the Director of Finance sat down on her soft, cream-colored leather sofa, she deliberately spread her legs for me. I could see she wore no undergarments and her trimmed auburn curls matched her hair.

"You are a pleasant looking young man," she said. "What is your name?"

"Sandro."

"Well, Sandro, I want you to take me," she said. A wry smile crossed her face. "I want you to take me like I have never been taken before. If you do, I will give you a position in my office. If you do not..." A threat hung in the air.

I was very afraid because I had very little experience pleasing a woman like the woman in front of me. I truly did not know what to do, so I said: "I will try."

The Director of Finance stood up and walked toward me. She put her hands on her hips and looked at me with disdain. "Try?" she said. "Trust me...I am sure you can do better than that."

I did not move. I did not say a word. I simply looked at my

face reflected in each lens of her glasses and prayed that I appeared to be calmer than I really was.

The Director of Finance took one step closer, then she slowly raised her skirt over her knees, up her thighs, over her sex to her waist. Then she pushed me onto my knees, grabbed my head and forced me down between her legs.

I took my cue from what Maria had done to please me. I let my lips worship her damp auburn curls while she moved in little circles against my face. As her movements grew faster and more intense, she wrapped her fingers in my hair and I let her direct my head where she wanted it, first back and forth on the insides of her thighs, then against the gateway between her legs, in more passionate movements while I let my tongue serve her pleasure.

When I entered her with my tongue, she cried out so loud I was certain her guards would investigate, but no one came to the door.

Instead, The Director of Finance dropped to her knees on the floor, turned around on all fours, and backed herself toward me. I continued my ministrations. Her cries turned to low sounds as I pulled back and began to kiss her skin. "Bite me," she commanded, so I did. "Harder," she said. When I bit her hard enough to leave marks on her right side, her body shook and trembled uncontrollably.

Then I reached up and held her waist while I pushed my tongue deeper. I experimented with movements, finding the rhythm that pleased her most; and The Director of Finance began to weep. Her body was wracked with sobs and her breathing came in deep gasps. Still, I held tightly to her waist and continued.

Finally she broke away from me, and crawled over to the circular stairway that led to her sleeping loft. I followed behind her, also crawling, my fingers sinking into the carpet, my legs shaking, my own breath uneven.

As I approached The Director of Finance, she began to climb up the steps with her hips still raised, her face turned to the side, her arms and her chest pressed against the steps while I followed, kissing her feet and legs.

When I finally caught up with her, I resumed my attentions, but she pushed me away.

"I want you inside me," she whispered. "Now, now. Come on, come on, come on, come on, Sandro."

I tried to stand on the stairway, but my knees were shaking, partly from the physical exertion, but also, still, from the fear that I could not give her what she wanted. My skin was cold and clammy. My member went soft. I felt faint, and I wanted to run over to the window, jump through it and float on the hot winds over the city until I landed with a sickening sound on the sweltering asphalt. Then my humiliation would be over. Finally. Forever.

But The Director of Finance would have none of that. She turned herself around, forced me against the steps, fell to her knees on a lower step and went to work on my nearly soft flesh. I closed my eyes. My nausea slowly receded as I hardened. Then The Director of Finance stopped.

I kept my eyes closed, awaiting the disappointed lecture, perhaps even the discipline, I was certain would result from my inadequacy. Instead, I felt her hands on my head; then the touch of fabric on my face. I was confused until I realized she had wrapped one of her stockings around my eyes. I was blindfolded. When I tried to open my eyes, I could see light, but that was all.

The Director of Finance moved back around in front of me, and I could tell from feeling her body that she had returned to her previous position, facing the stairs, her body arched. As I entered her, she whirled around and struck me very hard across the face. I stood still, not knowing what to do.

"Not there," she hissed, "Here, you fool, here!" She grabbed me and guided me to her other entrance. As she rotated, forcing me deeper, she moaned and began to chant:

"Higher, oh, oh, yes, make it higher, come on, come on..."

I pushed myself in as far as I could, and still the chant continued: "Please, please go even higher, oh, oh, yes, yes..." Sweat rolled down my forehead and dampened the stocking blindfold. I was terrified. There I was, as deep as I could go, and yet she wanted more. All I could think of was to move, to work as hard as I could and hope those actions would satisfy her. The Director of Finance thrashed about in ever increasing frenzy, but still she cried out: "Higher, higher, oh, oh, oh, yes, yes, yes..."

What to do? I threw every last ounce of my strength into my efforts, but as I intensified my work, it dawned on me that there seemed to be little connection between what I was doing and The Director of Finance's reactions. Since I knew I had no more to give, I decided to test my intuition. I relaxed almost completely.

It turned out I was right. My relaxed state did not affect The Director of Finance at all. She still screamed for things to go higher and higher. She pounded the steps with her fists, slowly and rhythmically at first, then with great fury and passion.

When I realized for certain that what I was doing had little effect on my partner, I was able to banish my terror and enjoy myself. Sweat rolled down my chest and belly and helped ease our joining. I chose a rhythm I could handle, one that gave me pleasure, and so I was able to find arousal myself.

And then, all of a sudden, The Director of Finance reached her peak. She beat on the steps so hard they vibrated, and she screamed "I cannot believe it went that high. Oh! Oh! Oooooooooh!..."

Then she pulled away from me, and dropped exhausted onto the steps, making soft sounds.

I was left standing there, wanting very badly to release myself, but uncertain of what my duties and responsibilities were. Trusting my instincts yet again, I told myself it was best to do nothing, so I waited, legs spread, for my arousal to recede.

It was not too long before I felt The Director of Finance's hands on my face. She leaned over me and, with amazing tenderness, removed my blindfold and covered my face with soft, wet kisses. I opened my eyes and found myself blinking into my own eyes reflected in her mirrored lenses.

"My baby," she softly said, "my darling little baby."

I let her make a fuss over me while I readjusted to the room. "You made everything rise," she said. "You were wonderful. The Great Eastern Markets hit 13,748 and 1/4!"

I frankly had no idea what The Director of Finance was talking about until I looked past the stairs and saw the flicker of the electronic screens. She had been watching them the entire time, and it was the numbers reflected there that had caused her to reach such a state.

I laughed quietly inside. My success had not depended on my efforts, but on financial speculations taking place in some far distant land. The Director of Finance, however, was more than happy to give me all the credit. She wrapped her fingers around the back of my head and pushed my face against her breasts.

"You have done well," she said, "very well indeed. I will not forget this, my little one. You will be rewarded."

And I was. The Director of Finance left me on the stairs and walked over to her alcove. She sat, naked, in front of the screen and entered a series of numbers into the machine.

I stared at The Director of Finance's bare back. I reckoned I could kill her easily. I thought about it. I wanted to. But I did not.

The Director of Finance ignored me and continued to enter information. Then she waited. Other numbers sent from somewhere else appeared on the screen, then she entered more information and began to laugh and clap her hands, delighted with herself.

"You now have a number," she said.

I was curious. "A number?"

"The number of your new Central ID card, the number for your new position on my staff, the number of your secret bank account into which I have just deposited a great deal of money."

I was truly taken aback. "Thank you," I said, sounding as obsequious as I could.

The Director of Finance laughed again. "Do not thank me," she said, "thank the man whose place you have just taken."

"And how should I thank him?" I asked.

The Director of Finance giggled in way that chilled me. "Well," she said, "that would be difficult...In fact, we might say it would be impossible." Then she giggled again.

Trying to please her, I said: "No, really, I would like to thank him."

The Director of Finance cocked her head to the side, and her face again became a mask beneath her dark glasses, but her voice adequately conveyed her intent. "You underlings are so stupid," she said. "Do you not understand?"

"No," I said, "I am sorry. I do not understand."

"I just deleted him," she said.

At that point, my jaw dropped and The Director of Finance seemed very pleased by my reaction because she laughed even harder. Her glasses bounced around on her nose and her body swayed back and forth. "He..." she said, and then she broke into her maniacal giggle, "He could not..." The Director of

Finance was having so much fun she could barely get the words out, "He could not perform anymore!"

The laughter continued for some time, echoing through the apartment like the sound of breaking glass. I stood there on the stairs, naked and powerless, watching a woman celebrate the deletion of a human being for the crime of impotence. And in that moment I understood what Maria had been trying to tell me about power and those who wielded it. They were not human anymore. They had become something else, something monstrous.

When The Director of Finance finally stopped laughing, she turned back to her screens and waved her hand at me dismissively. "You may go now," she said. "Report to my office tomorrow at the eighth hour. Someone will show you what to do."

I gathered my clothes and dressed quickly, wanting nothing more than to leave that place. As I descended the stairs and walked toward the door, I looked back once at The Director of Finance, still naked, still staring at her screens, her fingers dancing across the keys as she deleted and created lives with equal indifference.

Outside, the night air was still hot and thick, but it felt clean after the oppression of that apartment. I walked through the empty streets of Central City, my new ID card in my pocket, my new position secured, and the full weight of what I had become settling on my shoulders like a burial shroud.

Rain

Chapter Three: Mystery

Many things cannot be explained. There is, in fact, a shadow world. There are unsolved mysteries, and some beings are more than they at first appear to be. This shadow world is populated by angels, devils and assorted other spirits. They mean neither good fortune nor harm, but in carrying out their own affairs, they inevitably collide with events taking place in our dimension. Sometimes they even bump against our best-laid plans.

Maria had never assumed I would get so close to the center so quickly. Although I expressed frustration when I told her I did not take advantage of my opportunity to kill The Director of Finance, she heard my story from a different perspective. She was astonished by my good judgment and temperance, and she congratulated me on my success.

"But I should have killed her," I said. "But I have never...it was just...too hard. And she was laughing..."

"No, no," said Maria. "Killing her would have ruined everything. You acted wisely, courageously. I am very proud of you." She kissed me and rested her head on my chest. "But," she said, "you are now in serious danger."

"What danger? She is crazy about me."

Maria could not suppress a smile. "Have you already forgotten?"

"What she did...you mean the deletion?"

"And what she can...will do to you."

"Yes, I guess she will, when I cannot perform. But I will perform, Maria, I will perform if it is important."

"Oh Sandro," said Maria, and she smiled again. "I have few doubts you will. But do you really believe your joining made the markets rise?"

"Maybe," I said, "of course I do not really know. Madame Director said it was true, but I do not..." I stopped and thought about the possibility for a minute. "Could it be true?"

"Perhaps, but you would probably have to be The Chosen One to perform that miracle," said Maria.

"The Chosen One?"

"It is said: The rains will return and the people will rise up and the Evil will disappear from the land when a prophet emerges from the underclasses, and that prophet shall be known as The Chosen One."

"Do you believe that?"

"That he will arrive? Yes. That he will manipulate financial markets? Well, we shall see. But for now, we need to protect you from this woman's power."

And so Maria took me to visit La Bruja, a great witch who lived in the dusty foothills, along an arroyo thick with cactus and creosote, in a small dark cabin covered with dried, sunburned vines and surrounded by dying cottonwoods. The journey took us half a day through the parched landscape, past abandoned farms and empty villages where the drought had driven everyone away.

La Bruja met us at her door. She wore black with a colorfully embroidered vest and soft velvet shoes in forest green and rust red burgundy. Her body was decorated with gold jewelry, long dangling earrings forged from ancient coins, wrist and ankle bracelets, rings on every finger formed in the shapes of different fierce animals. One plain gold loop hung in her right nostril, larger golden loops pierced each of her nipples and a silver stud glistened in her navel.

She was a small woman, short but not thin, with milky

white skin, covered by thick, coarse black hair on her head, arms, legs and sex. Her eyes were such a dark brown they appeared black; her nose and ears and mouth were all quite large for her face. Her breasts were long and flat and hung low on her chest. She had wide hips and stocky, muscled legs.

"You," she said pointing to Maria, "wait here." Then she signaled for me to enter.

I followed La Bruja inside and, as Maria had instructed me to do, I asked La Bruja for a talisman to protect me from the Central Director of Finance's power, a talisman that would even allow me to face the Supreme Leader himself and not be afraid, a talisman that would make me strong in the face of evil.

When I told La Bruja my request, she balked. "This is not easy to do," she said. "And you ask me for powers you have not yet earned."

Maria had also told me to say, "But I will need your magic now, before I begin my quest, in order to fulfill a greater, higher mission later on."

"That would probably be to your advantage," said La Bruja. "Although I do not know what your mission is. Why do you need such special magic?" She looked me over carefully, walking around me in a slow circle, studying me from all angles. "I wonder," she said, "can you handle the power you request? Looking at you, I am not so impressed."

Maria had warned me La Bruja would treat me that way, so I responded as Maria had instructed me to respond. I said, "You are right. I am nothing. I only wish to be your vessel, and I will act only as you allow me to act. I am yours."

Maria's instructions were correct. My answer pleased La Bruja. She told me to sit on the dirt floor of her cabin and drink a gelatinous, grainy liquid with a thin brown film floating on the top. I knew that for La Bruja's power to work I had to give myself over to her without question, so I drank from the cup.

When I finished the liquid, my fingers became numb and the cup fell from my hand. I remember my brain seemed to shut down although I could certainly see my skin turn green and become freckled with little purple spots. I could not breathe. Tiny orange lights danced in front of my eyes. At the moment when I was certain I was going to lose consciousness, a somewhat pleasant, warm sensation began in my stomach and slowly spread throughout my body. My skin tingled. My member became rigid and grew larger than it ever had in even my most fantastic adolescent imaginings.

La Bruja then threw two different yellow powders onto the smoldering logs in her fireplace. The cabin filled with a thick blue smoke that smelled of camphor and dead fish. When the smoke cleared, the logs burst into flames and La Bruja danced in small uneven circles while she chanted incantations to the unseen.

"Gods of the Reckoning, Prophets of The Ecstasy, Dark Shadows of Doom, surround Sandro and make him UnSeen. Wyudrluck froidb noutra quoondoos..."

I was mesmerized by La Bruja's giant dancing shadow reflected onto her cabin's walls by the flickering firelight. Her movements were slow and deliberate, punctuated by feverish leaps and convulsions. She kept her body so coiled and low to the ground, her calves and thighs were hard and smooth and rounded as if she were sculpted in marble.

Then she approached me from my right side, leaned down and whispered in my ear, "Fear us oh mortal one, fear us or you shall pay...splintasha wyondata recrinta..." Then she danced around behind my back and appeared at my left side where she bit into my neck hard enough to draw blood. Then she lapped up my blood with her tongue, moved in front of me and knelt down in the dirt.

"Do you feel the powers behind the power?" she asked as she stared into my eyes. Suddenly, there was a painful, high-pitched ringing in my ears. I tried to respond, but I could not speak.

La Bruja frowned, looked perplexed for a moment and then screamed something. The ringing stopped. "I am sorry. I forgot to change the spell...Anyway, you can speak now," she said.

I was sure she was wrong because the ringing immediately returned, but when I opened my mouth, my words did come out. "Yes," I said, "I feel the powers behind the power."

"Touch me," she said. She lifted her skirt, and pointed to her sex. "Touch me here. Put your fingers inside me. I am wet; I am ready. Oh, what the hell, put your whole hand inside me. Now, now, Sandro."

I reached into her wet bush and touched her opening. With my right hand I held apart the folds protecting her entrance, then I let three fingers of my left hand slip inside her. She tore open her vest, and the buttons flew into the corners of the room. She grabbed each of her breasts by her nipple rings, pulled them to her lips and alternately drew on one then the other. Then she held them out toward me. "Suck these," she said, "suck them, suck them, suck them."

I lowered my head to her breasts and took the nipples into my mouth.

"Pull on them," she said. I grabbed her left peak between my thumb and forefinger. "Squeeze!" she screamed. I pinched hard on her left nipple above and below the golden ring. La Bruja shook. I did the same with her right nipple. She shook again.

"Move your fingers," she said. I moved my fingers around inside her. "No, no!" She moved her hips back and forth. "Push, push hard...hard inside me."

I tried, but no matter how hard I pushed, La Bruja thrust

even harder and faster. "Put your hand in me, push, push, yes, yes, that is it, push...faster...faster...oh, oh...faster, harder... faster, bite me, join with me, take me."

The more I worked, the faster she moved. Her body hairs all stood on end. Her face was contorted. Her muscles bulged. Still she increased the pace, until she was totally lost in the motion. Saliva ran down her chin. She exhaled forcefully through her flared nostrils.

As she began her first of many peaks, she moved away from me and leapt into the air, pleasuring herself in such a mad frenzy I feared she would be hurt. She whirled and leapt and tumbled around her room. She screamed and shrieked. Fluids continued to flow from her mouth and her nose. When she shook, the secretions sprayed off of her.

Then her breathing slowed. Her movements were less erratic, more rhythmic, and the only noise was the crackling from the fire.

Ever so slowly, La Bruja's energy returned. She advanced across the dirt floor toward me, and when she was next to me, she reached up, put the palm of her hand against my forehead and pushed me backwards. "Lie down," she said.

I allowed myself to fall into the dust, and she climbed atop my still-rigid, enlarged member. The hair on her legs was soft against my thighs. She cupped her breasts in her hands and drew on them gently, carefully, deliberately, occasionally running the tip of her tongue through her nipple rings. Her screams turned to insistent little cries.

La Bruja rode me like that for an hour or so, never fast enough to make me release, never slow enough to make me lose interest. She knew how to make the tight muscles within her stroke me and release me, stroke me and release me. She rocked and swayed, swayed and rocked, and very, very slowly increased the rotation in her hips, the length of time her muscles held tight to me, the frequency with which she drew on her own breasts.

Eventually I felt her begin to ride me toward her final climax. Faster and faster; she dug her heels into my side, she struck her own buttocks, she let her breasts fall free, move up and down and slap against her body. Again the convulsions came, but she did not pull away. She rode me even harder. She screamed and took to ranting and raving in one of her incomprehensible languages.

And then I realized I was moving with her. I was in perfect union with her, pushing her even harder and faster. I lifted my own hips so high off the ground La Bruja had to grab my shoulders to balance herself. She rode me in the air, screaming and exhaling and pushing me until my shouts drowned out even hers, and my convulsing spurts emptied me of any strength that remained.

When we were finished, La Bruja turned away from me and stared into the embers smoldering in her fireplace. "I was wrong about you," said La Bruja, "You make very powerful magic, Sandro."

"It was your potion," I said.

La Bruja spit into the fire. "My potions only work on what already exists. There is something about you..."

Then La Bruja stood, collected my seed from her opening and placed the drops in a small green vial. Then she took a very sharp knife and shaved a dozen hairs from around her sex. She took her hairs and a pinch of the yellow powder she had thrown on the fire, the dregs from the magic potion, her saliva and a few flecks of dried skin she scraped off the bottoms of my feet. Then she ground them together in a paste, and forced the paste into the vial. Then she wrapped the vial in a small yellow pouch. She closed the pouch with a long leather thong.

"This will protect you," she said as she opened my shirt and placed the pouch around my neck.

I looked down at my member. Although it was no longer erect, it remained considerably larger than it had been before I drank the potion. "Will...will this stay like this?" I asked.

"That is part of the magic," said La Bruja. "Are you not pleased?"

"It no longer seems part of me," I said.

"You are indeed very strange," said La Bruja. "No man has ever before complained."

"Maria did not tell me..."

"She could not have told you what she did not know," said La Bruja. She seemed confused. "You are certainly not like the others."

"What do you mean? What others?"

La Bruja chose not to answer. Instead, she warned me: "You are protected now, but you are not safe."

"If I am not safe, then what good is this magic?"

"No one is completely safe in these times..."

"What power could be stronger than your magic, La Bruja?"

"The sun burns in a cloudless sky; water is scarce; plants burn out and die."

"That is only because there is a drought," I said.

"A drought?" La Bruja snorted. "You think a drought that lasts 1,692 Days is just a drought?"

"I do not know," I said. "Maria says..."

"Maria knows this is no drought..."

"What is it, then?"

"You will know soon enough. If you accept your mission, the power and magic of others will be arrayed against you."

"Whose power?"

"Ask Maria. I dare not say, but come with me."

La Bruja took my hand and led me from her cabin. At first

the old cottonwoods provided a measure of protection, but soon my eyes hurt and my head was pounding as we walked in the bright sunlight and dusty grit along the arroyo. Suddenly we stopped at the edge of the embankment that ran alongside La Bruja's cabin. We stood, for a moment, in a patch of scrub brush and prickly pear, then La Bruja said: "Go on, jump in."

It was not a great height, but high enough. My legs shook and my stomach rolled over.

"Men have no faith," La Bruja said in disgust. In one quick movement she slipped behind me and pushed me. I felt myself falling through the air, then I heard a splash when I landed.

I opened my eyes and realized I was underwater. I extended my arms and swam toward the light. When I reached the surface, La Bruja was in the stream next to me.

Except it was not really La Bruja. The woman La Bruja had become was laughing. Her eyes were bright and shining; her features in perfect proportion.

The banks of the stream were shaded by bamboo and large green trees in full leaf. There were clouds in the sky. The air was humid; the smells of growing and rotting things assaulted my senses. Birds sang in the branches overhead. Insects hummed through the thick air. The water was cool and clear, moving over smooth stones.

The woman swam over to me, grabbed my head and pulled my face to hers. She kissed me fiercely on the lips. At first I was aroused, then I became alarmed when I began to slip beneath the surface. I looked into the woman's laughing eyes, and I realized she was not going to let go.

I struggled, but the woman was stronger. I gave in to her will, and the water closed over my head.

When I opened my eyes again, I was standing in the bottom of the hot, barren, dusty arroyo. La Bruja's features appeared as they had been before we went for our swim.

"This is incredible," I said. "There is water after all."

"Yes," said La Bruja, "there is water."

"But where? Where is it hidden?"

"In the place where all hidden things dwell," said La Bruja. "In the shadow world, the world behind this world. The water has not gone away, Sandro. It has been taken."

"Taken? By whom?"

"By those who have the power to take it. Now go. Maria is waiting. And Sandro," she added as I began to walk away, "be careful with the magic I have given you. It is both a gift and a burden. Use it wisely, or it will consume you."

I nodded and made my way back to where Maria waited by the dying cottonwoods. The talisman felt warm against my chest, and my enlarged member felt strange and heavy between my legs. I had come to La Bruja seeking protection, and I had received it. But I had also received something else, something I did not yet understand, a glimpse of a truth that made the world seem both larger and more dangerous than I had ever imagined.

Rain

Chapter Four: Intelligence

Smart people assume they are better than anyone else. Smart people give direction, advice and counsel about everyone else's affairs, although there is no evidence they have any greater insights into what will work than stupid people have. Still smart people churn out publications, make speeches, do research and consult. We, in turn, read the publications, listen to the speeches, apply the research and bring their consultive advice to bear on our lives. Maybe our willingness to take them so seriously is what makes smart people appear to be smart and the rest of us stupid, but the intelligent pay a high price for their constant self deception.

When I returned and told Maria about my experiences with La Bruja, her first reaction was to try out my new member, and she did find it much to her liking; but she was even more excited by the news of my brief conversations with the witch.

"La Bruja really said, 'You are not like the others.'"

"Yes, what did she mean by that?"

"And she told you there is water?"

"She proved it."

"I cannot believe this is happening," said Maria. "This is very important...very important."

"La Bruja also said you would tell me about the others whose magic is even more powerful than mine."

Maria hesitated. "I do not...know what she is talking about."

"She said you would."

"Then I do not know that I know," said Maria with a frown

that was meant to shut off further discussion.

One day later, I started my new job in the offices of the Central Director of Finance. My title was Third Level Guardian of the Central Core, which meant I sat in a gray uniform on a couch outside the offices of Madame Director, and ran whatever errands The Director of Finance's various assistants asked me to run.

I assumed, of course, that my duties also included occasional 'manipulations of financial markets,' although I was not called upon to do so after that first time in The Director of Finance's apartment.

A month passed, and nothing happened. I complained to Maria that I was further removed from the flow of interesting and important information than I was when I worked at the Number One Cafe Bar & Grill. Maria counseled me to be patient, then she again tested my magic power to make certain it had not diminished. It had not.

Maria's counsel was correct. The very next day, The Second Assistant to the Assistant Director told me to pick up a manila folder from the offices of The Central Authoritarian. His orders were to personally receive the packet from the hands of The Publisher.

The Central Authoritarian's building was five kilometers across Central City from the Finance Directorate. As I walked the streets in my uniform, I was approached by numerous filthy beggars, lonely people living in the streets, and thin, frightened mothers with weak, even starving children.

On one corner a tiny child held tightly with one hand to a little green and yellow tattered umbrella while she held out the other, palm up, begging, from strangers, for money to eat. She wore dirty red leggings, a faded yellow shirt and a torn, white vest with silver spangles. The right side of the little girl's face had been burned from above the hairline all the way down her neck. Her left foot was wrapped in soiled bandages. When her eyes locked on mine, I reached into my pocket, pulled out a handful of coins and gave them to her.

The growing threat of popular revolt or even terrorist attack meant there were extensive security precautions around The Publisher's building. There were surveillance apparati everywhere. Coded locks protected all the doors. The guards were armed, and leashed attack dogs wandered the hallways. But The Authoritarian's offices showed no physical signs of the hard times I had clearly left behind when I entered the luxurious lobby. The marble columns glistened, the brass fixtures were polished and the crystal chandeliers refracted a thousand points of light shining through cut glass.

When I reached The Publisher's office I was told to wait outside, then, a few moments later, I was ushered into a cavernous room where The Publisher sat at an enormous ancient wooden desk. The legs were intricately carved, polished works of art that ended in lions' heads sitting atop a thick wine-colored carpet.

The Publisher, who was rumored to have tested at a +183 intelligence level, not only headed up the Central Authorities' primary communications organ, she also advised the Supreme Leader and other princes, presidents and the chief executives of numerous worldwide commercial enterprises. She was very tall and very thin. She had curly, light brown hair, hazel eyes, a large nose, thin lips, a narrow neck, no breasts to speak of, a tight, rounded little bottom and long elegant legs. Her voice carried a touch of irony, although her facial expressions were unusually serious. She wore thin, wire-framed glasses, richly decorated designer blouses and flowing skirts. Her skin was golden and her hair was tinted to reflect the bleached colors of the high desert.

Her office had no windows and there were no decorations on

the walls. There were books and journals everywhere: spread out on her desk, on the floor surrounding an overstuffed easy chair, alongside a couch which was pushed back against another wall, and stacked on the shelves of the breakfront that ran the full length of the wall behind her.

"I was told to personally receive the material," I said as I stood in front of her desk. "It is for The Director of Finance."

"Ah yes, our beloved Director of Finance," said The Publisher. "She is still beloved is she not?"

I definitely felt trapped by that question.

The Publisher ignored the packet sitting on her desk and instead appeared to spend her time observing me. I stood, impassively, waiting to be dismissed.

"Does your silence mean she is not beloved by you?" She finally ventured.

I remembered my talisman and knew I could lie convincingly. "Yes, she is, of course beloved."

"She is? Good, although that makes you somewhat unique."

"Why do you say that?" I asked.

"Well, what does it matter?" said The Publisher. "You will soon go the way of all the others."

The Publisher waited to see what reaction her comment would have on me, but I remained calm. For some reason my demeanor seemed to make The Publisher more curious. She stood, reached for the folder and leafed through the contents. Then she stared at me over her glasses which had slipped down her nose. "Do you know what this package contains?"

"No," I said. "Of course not."

"What is your name?"

"Sandro."

"So Sandro, do you work for the underground?"

I thanked the gods Maria had sent me to La Bruja. "The what?"

"Of course, how foolish of me. You have no knowledge of the underground and you have absolutely no desire to overthrow the Central Authorities. You are just a delivery boy."

"A Third Level Guardian of the Central Core," I reminded her.

"Charming," said The Publisher. She returned to perusing the papers she held in her right hand. With her left, she unbuttoned her shirt and traced patterns on the very swollen nipple of her tiny right breast.

"Life is complicated, Sandro, very complicated. Very complex. Answers are not easy to come by. Sometimes...sometimes I get so tired." She threw the file of papers down on her desk and walked around her barren room. "I am exhausted, blocked. I cannot think. It all becomes one huge blur. Sometimes I think I am losing my mind. I need to be released."

"I am sorry," I said.

"How sweet," she said. She sat back down and held out her hand. "Come, come and rub my shoulders. Help me relax."

I reluctantly moved behind The Publisher's chair and put my hands on her shoulders. She sighed and lowered her head onto her hands. Then I pressed my fingers more deeply into the muscles just above her collarbone. She groaned, then a sharp yelp of pain escaped her lips. "Pig," she said, "slowly! Slowly, at first."

I moved my fingers slowly around her upper back. Her neck was gnarled and hard, her vertebrae bent and twisted. I tried to imagine the horrors her brain had wreaked on her body as I moved my fingers through her hair, across her scalp along her temples. I touched the wire frames behind her ears, then pulled her glasses back and off her nose. I rubbed behind her ears and along the bridge of her nose. Then, when she was calmed down, relaxed, I really went to work.

First, I pressed my thumbs deeply into the muscles at the

base of her neck and held them there until she sighed. Her flesh was soft, but the muscles underneath were taut and rigid. I moved my thumbs a few centimeters out toward her arms and pressed until she groaned. I immediately released my hands, then slowly pressed again. She sighed with relief as the pain bottled up inside her diminished.

I repeated the process until I reached the top of her shoulders. Once there, I lowered my head and licked and bit the soft skin at the top of each arm. Then I slowly kissed and licked along her collarbone back toward her neck. When I reached her backbone, I returned to pressing my thumbs deeply into her flesh. Her groans were increasingly rhythmic and sensual. She grabbed and pinched her nipples. Her voice lowered to a whisper. She breathed much more slowly.

I continued to work on her neck and shoulders, alternating between pressuring and nuzzling, between work and pleasure. Her chin dropped onto her chest, and her head swayed back and forth in time with her breathing.

Then I lifted her out of her chair, removed her already unbuttoned blouse and placed her on her stomach on the carpet. I straddled her buttocks and made my hands into fists. I pressed my fists along the edge of her spine at the top of her back. When she exhaled I let my weight press down on my fists. There was an audible crack, followed by a groan and a whimper. I released, moved my fists a little lower and, as she exhaled, pressed again. Again there was a cracking sound. At each point along her spine, I was able to release the incredible tension in her back. When I reached the bottom, I licked her tail bone and continued licking all the way up to her neck.

Then I spread my hands across her shoulder blades and rolled her back muscles. The muscles finally yielded beneath my fingers, but as she relaxed, The Publisher began to push her buttocks up against my groin. I did my best to keep my enhanced member from growing while I continued my work on her back, kneading her smooth, soft flesh, kissing and biting the folds of skin raised by my fingers, licking along her vertebrae and tail bone, but her movements made it difficult for me to keep control of myself.

When I finished with The Publisher's back, I loosened her skirt and pulled it down across her legs until it lay in a crumpled heap at her feet. Then I removed her pure white undergarments, flicked them over her heels and threw them onto a pile atop her skirt. I knelt beside her naked body and gazed upon her tingling back, her reddening buttocks, her trembling legs.

But The Publisher could not, or would not, look at me, so I started to really work on her bottom. I pressed and pressured her flesh until it turned an even brighter red. Then I used the edges of my hands to drop rapid little strikes across her flesh down onto her thighs, back to her bottom, down her thighs, down and back, down and back. She spread her legs slightly and swayed back and forth. I adjusted my pace to her swaying, and timed my movements to coordinate with the undulations of her body.

When the skin on her bottom was crimson, I changed the angle of my hands, spread out my palms and firmly struck The Publisher with my open hand. Her body responded. I continued which became even more firm and aggressive. She cried out and squirmed. Waves of pleasure rippled up and down her skin from her head to her toes. She ground her sex into the carpet and circled her hips round and round.

When I continued, The Publisher became even more involved. Her bottom rose into the air. Then her moans were punctuated by confessional cries:

"Punish me. Hurt me, hurt me, please! I am so stupid, but no one knows that. I am so bad. Oh. Oh. Yes, hurt me, punish me, please, Sandro, please."

Her groans and yelps were replaced with high-pitched moaning which reverberated off the bare walls of her office and rang in my ears.

"Everyone thinks I know what to do, Sandro, but I do not. The pain, the loss, we are...Oh yes, that is it, Sandro, yes, yes, again, again, yes, again, harder...

"I did not mean for things to turn out this way...not this way. It was supposed to be simple...It was not in the plan, I swear... why can I not see clearly anymore! Why can I not see, Oh yes, yes, why can I not...uh, yes, end...Ohmygod, mygod, end it? I am so sorry, sososososo soooorrry!"

She cried and wept and shook her head from side to side. Her body convulsed in its sorrow, the muscles on her back tightened up again, her arms tensed and the veins bulged on the surface of her skin. Her leg muscles cramped and went into spasms.

Despite her passion and my own arousal, I was very upset when I realized she was confessing her crimes against the people. It was very clear she knew what she had done. It dawned on me that she was, perhaps, even the brain behind the Central Plan. That idea totally disgusted me, and although she was begging forgiveness, she was really only talking to herself, and I might as well have not existed. As if to prove my point, she still refused even to look at me.

I became enraged. I wanted to hurt her. I held nothing back. I struck her even harder. I found a measuring stick on her desk and used it on her. As the full force of my blows landed on her swollen buttocks, she cried out:

"Thank you, thank you for this pain...oh, oh I am damned, damned for sure, damned because I caused...evil to be....Now I cannot even look at this world I helped create, Sandro, what... what sins...what sins...what goddamned, terror...sins... no, no... punish me, punish......me!"

I put down the stick, removed my belt from my uniform and brought it down full force across her bottom. I wanted to break the skin to see her bleed; I wanted her to suffer as she had made so many others suffer. I watched the leather raise ugly red and purple welts, and I felt satisfaction.

But the pain did not hurt her, or more accurately, her pain melded into pleasure and she experienced a climax both extraordinary and frightening in its intensity. She jerked and convulsed and twisted and shook. She howled another ear-piercing plea for forgiveness, broke her nails scratching the floor and struck her head against the wall until she collapsed.

Afterward, her exhausted, wounded body lay limply on the floor. Her tears continued to flow, but her shrieking and wailing were reduced to a simple, sad crying, punctuated by the occasional sob.

I looked at the wounds on The Publisher's bottom and I honestly felt a great deal of satisfaction. She, however, appeared to remain indifferent. She grabbed a corner of the hem of her skirt and clenched it in her fist. Then she pulled her fist to her mouth, placed her thumb between her lips and fell asleep.

I made certain she was really asleep, then I moved over to her desk and picked up the pile of papers I was supposed to bring back to The Director of Finance. It was a manuscript entitled, Deprivation And Denial: An Analysis Of The Subjugation Of The Lower Peoples Through Aqueous Minimization.

I sat in The Publisher's chair and turned to the next page. It was blank! So was the next page. And the next. I quickly shuffled through the document, and, except for the title page, it was entirely blank! There was not one word in the entire document.

At first I wondered if it had been written with some sort of disappearing ink. Then I considered whether I should take the file anyway, or leave it and pretend The Publisher had told me the material was not ready yet. I placed the file back on The

Publisher's desk and thought about my choices. Should I awaken her? I wished I could ask Maria what to do. I simply did not have any answers.

Suddenly, I was startled by The Publisher's voice: "Deliver it as it is."

I stumbled out from behind The Publisher's desk and sat down on the floor next to her. She repeated what she had said: "Deliver it as it is..." and added, "I have nothing more to say."

"But...but what will happen to you? What will happen to me when they see this?"

"I am not concerned for myself, and I do not see why anything should happen to you."

Despite my opinion of her, I chose to be bold: "You could be of great help to us. You know so many things."

The Publisher chuckled. She understood. "If I am so smart why did I believe you when you said you were not in the underground?"

"You had no choice. My magic talisman forces you to believe me."

"Cute. Very cute."

She tried to sit up, but she was too sore. "Oh, Sandro. You worked me over pretty well. You were wonderful."

"If you will just help us, I promise I will be wonderful anytime you need it."

"You want me to simply walk out of here with you? Do you think a Member of The Inner Circle just walks out the door with a Third Level Guardian of the Central Core?"

"I assume you can do whatever you want?"

The Publisher considered. "You are right," she agreed, "I can."

And so, on the 1,732nd Day of the Drought, she did.

Rain

Chapter Five: Truth

Truth is a rare and valuable jewel when it exists in a form simple enough to see it, but truth also sparkles with so many facets it is always difficult to perceive which angle best reflects the real truth.

When I first returned with The Publisher in hand, Maria was furious. She helped The Publisher get comfortable in a back room, then she came out and went after me. "First of all," she said, "what are we to do with her?"

"She is a member of the inner circle," I said. "Now she has come to our side! She must have some value to you, Maria."

"But you have also placed us in great danger, Sandro. The Publisher is a very powerful figure among the rulers. She is the only one who understands how to talk to the people. Her early writings were even..."

"Were what?"

"Good, sometimes kind. At one time, she cared about us."

"I do not believe that. This woman is a monster. She could never have loved the people. She wants to be punished. She concocted this entire drought. Her theories are the basis of the whole campaign to destroy resistance and establish complete domination."

"That is probably true."

"Well then, let us use her for what we can get out of her, and then..."

"Do not be so cold," said Maria. "What I am trying to say is, now that we do have her, what value does she have for us?

Does she really want to be on our side, or is she just tired of it all. When I know that, I will know what to do with her. In the meantime, she is truly dangerous to us. There will be a massive search to try to find her. A lot of people may die...By the way, how badly did you hurt her?"

"I beat her pretty hard," I said, "because she liked it. It was what she wanted. And I wanted to hurt her, but I could not really. She likes pain." I was angry. I ran my fingers through my hair. "Her memories are destroying her. That is the truth. She goes on about not being able to write or see things anymore, but I think she knows exactly what she is doing..."

"Well, I only wish I knew what she is doing now, Sandro," said Maria. "We are all of us finished if the Central Authorities find her here. And if we turn her over to our friends, they will..."

"Kill her?"

"They agree with you. They do not share my high opinion of her, Sandro."

"I think they are right, Maria. Believe me."

I was exhausted from my ordeal with The Publisher, and a little put out I had not been welcomed back as a hero. I went outside and sat under the stars while the desert winds blew through the deserted streets. Garbage, bits of paper, empty sacks, dead leaves, were all captured by the wind and scattered into doorways and alleys. The air was stale, heavy with dust and alkali.

My sinuses were all clogged up. My head throbbed. I knew I had done a dangerous thing, but I believed Maria should have thanked me. What did she want me to do, sit around all day in The Director of Finance's office and do nothing? I had brought in the biggest defector in the history of the rebellion and no one even cared. I sat there for what felt like hours, watching the sky begin its slow fade from black to deep purple, listening to the occasional sound of wagons in the distance.

Meanwhile, while I was sitting outside watching the wind blow and feeling sorry for myself, Maria went into the room where The Publisher was resting, and began to ask questions.

Maria later told me she started with flattery, and said something like, "I have always admired you from afar. When I was a young girl, I read your essays in the newspaper. They inspired me. You wrote about justice, about the dignity of the common people, about the responsibility of those in power to serve those they govern. I memorized whole passages. I believed every word."

The Publisher, like everyone in power, loved flattery. "That was so many years ago," she said, "before...before all of this..."

"I used to believe..." Maria said, "I used to dream that you..." Maria took a deep breath. "You were The Chosen One, that you would lead the rebellion."

"You were a foolish dreamer," said The Publisher. "But then you could not know how much I enjoyed the things...the things my position gave me." She turned away from Maria. "Anyway, what could I do? You really do not understand the power of the inner circle."

"You do not understand the power of your words," said Maria. "If you had the courage to write against the terror, even now you could make things...better. Think about it..."

The Publisher winced, Maria noticed. Then The Publisher reached out and held Maria's hand in hers. She stroked Maria's fingers, brought Maria's hand to her cheek and looked directly into Maria's eyes. "What happened to you?"

"My family was killed..." Maria fought to hold back her tears. "My mother...my father, sisters, brothers...all...dead." She stopped trying to control herself. Tears flowed down her cheeks. "It happened when the authorities were cleansing the coastal villages."

The Publisher sighed. She had heard the story before; she had even told it and retold it many times, and from many different angles. "Why were you spared?"

"Luck, blind luck. I was away." Maria lowered her head and cried. The Publisher moved next to her and held Maria's head against her breast. She stroked Maria's hair, and ran her fingers across Maria's back.

Maria told me she actually did relax under The Publisher's touch. Then she asked, "Why did you leave your office with Sandro? Are you really returning to help us, to help the people?"

The Publisher lied. "When I tried to talk to him, to find out if he could lead me to the underground, he became frightened, then he beat me up. Afterwards, he threatened to kill me if I did not leave with him."

"That is not what he told me. He told me he only did what you wanted him to do."

"No woman wants to be beaten," said The Publisher.

"What do women want?" asked Maria.

"Kindness. A...a sweet, soft touch."

"Yes," said Maria, "that is true. Oh yes..."

After she had sweet talked her a little more, The Publisher raised Maria's head to hers and kissed her gently on the lips. Maria returned the kiss. She brushed her lips across The Publisher's cheeks, along her nose. She kissed The Publisher's eyes and licked The Publisher's ears, then her neck.

Then The Publisher brought Maria's face back to hers and again lavished her kisses on Maria's lovely lips.

Maria eagerly returned The Publisher's passion. After all, she was engaging with one of her childhood heroes. As her excitement grew, she extended her tongue and engaged The Publisher's tongue. Then Maria surrounded The Publisher's tongue with her lips and drew her deep inside her mouth. The Publisher moaned and unbuttoned Maria's blouse. She held Maria's breasts in her hands and caressed Maria's large brown nipples.

Maria continued her attentions to The Publisher's tongue and stroked The Publisher's thighs. Then she lowered her head, and, as she opened The Publisher's shirt, moved her tongue across The Publisher's small breasts. The Publisher's nipples were immediately hard. Maria took each one in her mouth and kissed the sweet, pink flesh.

When The Publisher felt Maria's tongue and teeth on her breasts, she arched her back and wrapped her fingers in Maria's curly black hair. Maria tenderly undressed The Publisher and laid her out onto soft pillows she had spread on the floor. She moved her probing tongue from The Publisher's breasts down to her belly and traced slow, sensuous circles around The Publisher's navel. Then she moved along the line of The Publisher's curls, teasing and playing with her.

The Publisher raised her hips in response to Maria's tongue. She smiled and patiently urged Maria down to her sex. She spread her legs and held Maria's face against her swollen pearl.

Maria let her tongue softly linger, then she pressed her tongue ever so gently against The Publisher. The Publisher moved across the floor, but she quickly realized the pain from Sandro's discipline made that impossible. She slowly lifted Maria's head. "I need to move on top of you," she whispered. "Sandro hurt me so."

Maria rolled over and easily lifted The Publisher on top of her. The Publisher knelt between Maria's legs and caressed her own breasts while she admired Maria's body. Maria watched The Publisher, and, looking directly into her eyes and touching her large brown peaks, pulled the tips of her own breasts to her face and licked herself while The Publisher, in turn, watched her.

The Publisher sighed, moaned and almost reached her peak as she watched Maria pleasure herself. She removed the rest of Maria's clothes, and lowered her mouth to Maria's wet curls, kissing and licking along Maria's inner thighs, across her pearl, down inside Maria's opening.

Maria melted when she felt The Publisher's tongue inside her. She raised her head and watched The Publisher worship her. She continued to caress herself. She raised her arms in the air, reached down and delicately ran her nails across The Publisher's back. The Publisher moved from side to side and then raised her hips into the air. It was then that Maria saw the red cuts, the welts and bruises on The Publisher's bottom.

For a moment, Maria was distracted. "Is this what Sandro did to you?" she murmured.

The Publisher raised her head from Maria's sex. Her chin glistened, and her eyes were half closed. "Men are such brutes," she whispered. "But I want you, Maria. I want you more than I have ever wanted anyone...ever." And with that, she returned to her worship of Maria's sex.

While all of this was going on in the back room, one of the Central Authority's heavy wagons rumbled by on the street in front of where I was sitting. I could see hands and arms reaching out through the bars of the dark cages, beseeching some unknown angel of mercy to save them. I heard what I thought were their moans and groans, and I felt so sorry for them.

But then, when the wagon had passed, I realized the noises were not coming from the vehicles heading for the camps, but from inside the building. Curious, I reentered the apartment.

The door to the back room was closed, so I put my ear against the wood. What I heard both amazed and excited me.

In fact, as I listened I pulled my enhanced member out of my pants and held it in my fist. Then I stroked myself in rhythm to the sounds from the other side of the door, and imagined pictures of the two women together.

Then I knelt down in front of the door and peeked through the keyhole. The Publisher's head was between Maria's legs, coaxing, teasing, bringing Maria to the edge, then pulling back.

Maria was in another world. The Publisher's tongue inspired her; she soared toward heights I had never before seen her experience. Her body trembled and quivered. Her hair curled into tight ringlets, her words caught in her throat and instead emerged as low sounds.

Finally, Maria could take no more. When The Publisher took Maria's pearl between her lips and engulfed her dark brown skin in her mouth, Maria cried out. The Publisher cupped Maria's buttocks in her hands, spread her as wide as she could and lifted Maria without releasing her mouth from Maria's sex.

Maria cried out again, and her body convulsed. Then The Publisher carefully lowered Maria back onto the floor, put her arms around her and held Maria's head against her breasts.

Maria made soft sounds, opened her eyes a little and kissed The Publisher. She placed her hand on The Publisher's curls and spread back the folds of The Publisher's opening. Maria brought her fingers to her mouth, licked them and then inserted her fingers into The Publisher.

The Publisher sighed, lifted one leg into the air and balanced her foot on Maria's waist. Maria continued to kiss The Publisher's nipples and gently massage her opening with her probing fingers. As The Publisher began to rock and sway from Maria's touch, Maria quickened her movements and worked her vibrating hand inside The Publisher. The Publisher jerked, once, twice, three times and then drenched Maria's hand with her fluids.

But Maria wanted more. She rolled over onto her back, lifted The Publisher's waist and brought The Publisher's sex over her mouth and extended tongue. The Publisher sighed and reached back so she could ease her fingers inside Maria's opening.

Then The Publisher stared down at Maria and ground herself against Maria's mouth so Maria was forced to insert her tongue inside The Publisher's opening while she pressed her nose against The Publisher's pearl. Then, while Maria was bringing The Publisher to yet another peak, The Publisher was intent on bringing Maria with her, as she probed and massaged Maria's sex with her fingers.

Meanwhile, I was working my member and was, myself, ready to release. When I saw how Maria and The Publisher were moving together, I bent my legs, squeezed tightly and stroked myself in long deep movements.

The two of them climaxed first. The Publisher raised herself from Maria's mouth, stood and furiously pleasured herself while she looked down on Maria's luscious body. Maria grabbed her own legs at the knees with one arm and thrust three of her fingers into her throbbing, wet opening while she rocked back and forth in abandoned ecstasy.

Obviously, I could not wait much longer. My member was straining, and I released with such tremendous force my seed shot across the room and splashed in a glistening white pool against the far wall. I opened my eyes in amazement and watched my essence slowly drip down the dusty, faded, flowered wallpaper onto the floor.

After I had rested for a few minutes, I opened the door and entered the back room. Maria and The Publisher were on the floor, their bodies wrapped around each other.

Maria saw me first. "Oh Sandro," she said, "how could I have been so wrong about you?"

I said: "Maria, what are you talking about?"

"Tell him to leave," said The Publisher as she nuzzled Maria's neck.

"Leave us alone...Now!" said Maria.

I could not figure what Maria was doing, but I trusted her, so I walked out of the apartment into an empty street lit only by the dim light which appears just before dawn. The sky was beginning to show streaks of pale orange at the horizon, and a few early birds had begun their songs. The city was still sleeping, but it would not sleep much longer.

I had not walked more than a kilometer before two policemen stepped out of a darkened alley and headed toward me. I tried to slip into an abandoned building, but they had seen me. Since they were only four or five meters away, I saw no point in trying to run.

The taller policeman approached me first. His weapon was aimed at my chest. The other policeman dropped into a crouch and pointed his weapon at my head.

The tall policeman told me to place my hands on the wall of the building and spread my legs. Then the other policeman moved forward and searched me for weapons or contraband. When he found nothing, he ordered me to turn around and face him.

"It is not yet dawn," said the tall policeman. "You know you are not supposed to be out."

Since I was still in the uniform of a Third Level Guardian of the Central Core, I smiled and tried to look relaxed. I said: "I need to be at work early today."

"Check his papers," said the other policeman.

I fumbled about, looking for my identity card, then I remembered I had left it in the apartment. "I...I do not have any identification," I said, feebly.

The tall policeman laughed. "I suppose you left it at home?"

I thought about Maria and The Publisher. "No, it is not at home. I am sure of that."

The other policeman was eager. "Let us arrest him."

"Please," I said, "that is not necessary. I must have lost it. I promise I will get another as soon as I get to work."

But the policemen were not interested in my pleas for mercy. "Arrest him," the shorter one growled.

The tall policeman agreed. "On this, the 1,733rd Day of the Drought," he said, "you are charged with breaking curfew and impersonating a Third Level Guardian of the Central Core. Do you wish to say anything before we take you to the station?"

"No," I said, "no...I have nothing to say."

And so I was arrested, bound with restraints and placed in the back of a police wagon. As we moved through the empty predawn streets of Central City, I wondered if Maria knew what she was doing, if The Publisher could be trusted, and if I would ever see freedom again. The talisman hung warm against my chest, but I had no idea if its magic could protect me from what was coming. The wagon rumbled on, and through the barred window I could see the first true light of day breaking over the mountains beyond the city.

Rain

Chapter Six: Fear

Fear is our most ancient and powerful emotion. Fear makes our hair stand on end, our muscles contract. We sweat, our eyes shift back and forth, up and down. Our mouths are dry as we prepare to flee into the tall grass or the deep forest. We say we fear many things: loneliness, pain, illness, abandonment. All these things are terrible, but what we really fear is death. Death is the end.

The Inquisitor was death.

She wore black from head to toe: leather knee-length boots, black stockings, a black silk thigh-high skirt, black leather cowhide belt with a black saddle leather holster, a black 9mm pistol, black latex halter top, black leather jacket, black earrings, black lipstick and a black leather cap.

Her hair was snow white; her eyes clear blue. She was almost two meters tall, with very wide shoulders and enormous breasts. She had thick, pouting lips and a large nose. Her face was set in a perpetual sneer, and, despite her obvious beauty, she possessed a cold, distant cruelty that immediately put me on edge. And my reaction was appropriate because The Inquisitor was the Chief Investigator for the Interior Police.

She worked out of The Central Police Station, a brightly-lit, simple, glass and steel edifice which I entered with the two policemen. We then walked through an ornate marble-floored lobby to a reception desk. It was all very civilized.

The police had me fill out certain forms, after which they put me into an elevator, and then they took me to the 27th floor. The elevator was also very quiet and they did not say one word to me, so I was unprepared for the pandemonium that broke out when the doors opened on the infamous 27th.

My guards who had been cold but polite up to that point, pitched me out of the elevator onto the cement floor, then they closed the doors and returned, without me, to the first floor.

I barely even noticed I had scraped my knees when I landed on the concrete. They were bleeding, but the blood meant nothing next to the hellish heat that enveloped me. The Central Authorities provided no interior temperature control for that part of the building, and the 27th floor was even hotter than it had been outside.

But my most overwhelming and memorable impressions came from the incessant din. Men and women were screaming and cursing, all at once and as loud as their voices would allow. There were scraping and breaking and ripping and tearing sounds. There were banging and slamming and slapping and punching noises. There was the sweet stench of burning flesh, the sour acidic smell of urine, the rich, heavy, putrid scent of feces.

Then, just as my senses began to adapt to the bedlam around me, I felt a whip's sting on my buttocks. I looked over my shoulder and saw a guard dressed in gray leather boots, gray leather shorts and nothing else. The guard motioned for me to follow him, and, because I was terrified, I did.

We walked down a dark interior corridor past numerous rooms. Some rooms had open doors; others did not. From what I saw of the things going on in the rooms that did have opened doors, I did not want to guess what went on behind the closed ones.

We arrived at The Inquisitor's office at the end of the corridor. Her anteroom was very clean and simple, steel, glass, stone, tanned leather and natural wood. Traditional music played from unseen places.

The Inquisitor's assistant was a middle-aged, handsome woman with a nice figure and an Outlander's accent. She apparently found nothing strange in my appearance despite my tattered government uniform, and she told me to sit in a comfortable chair.

I expected to be there for a long time, at least as long as we made people sit in the Finance Directorate, but it was only a few minutes before The Inquisitor's assistant told me to enter the inside office.

I found myself directly in front of The Inquisitor's desk, a massive iron table with a central pedestal carved from black onyx. The walls of the office were ten-meter-high translucent construction blocks. Every two meters, the translucence was bisected by alternating red and black, floor-to-ceiling velvet banners. There was a low, rough stone bench in front of the desk. I was told that was where I was to sit, so again I decided to go along and do as I was told.

When The Inquisitor entered dressed in her black outfit with her white hair, I involuntarily stood up. I really could not help myself because the entire scene was so striking, the light shining through the glass walls, the room itself, that extraordinary woman.

But standing up was the wrong move. The Inquisitor walked over to me and struck me so hard she knocked me onto the floor. Then she sat on top of her desk, facing me, with her legs spread apart. She wore no undergarments, so I was staring at her curls which were as white as the hair on her head. "Never stand in my presence unless told to," she said in an unnaturally calm and pleasant voice. I nodded my head slowly as I rubbed my jaw.

"Go back to your bench," she added. I crawled over to

the bench.

The Inquisitor continued to look at me as if she were studying a new species of insect, and her attitude did manage to unsettle me which was what she intended I am sure. I was very nervous. "What do you want?" I asked.

That was my second big mistake. I was struck in the stomach and warned not to speak until spoken to. The Inquisitor went back to watching me, and I, not knowing what else to do, hung my head between my legs and waited.

Eventually she spoke: "So, you work for The Finance Directorate?"

"Yes," I said.

"Yet, you have no papers?"

"I have papers. I lost them."

"That is, in itself, an offense."

"Yes, I know that," I said.

"Do you have anything else to tell me?"

I sensed a trap, although I had no idea where the line of questioning was supposed to lead. "No."

"Nothing?"

I tried to make light of the situation. "Well, I am sorry I lost my papers."

A flash of anger shot across The Inquisitor's face. She headed toward me for a third time and I cringed, but she stopped, threw her hands in the air and went back to her desk. "Look," she said, "we can make this as simple, or as difficult, as you wish. We know everything anyway."

"Everything?" escaped my lips before I could stop myself.

She noticed my slip up, but appeared to ignore it. Instead she pulled some papers from her desk, read them, and then dropped them back on her table: "How well do you know The Director of Finance?"

"Not very well."

"When you first came here from the outlands, you were a very low-level clerk in the commercial district. For no apparent reason, you quit your job and became a waiter at the Number One Cafe Bar & Grill. Strange choice that. Even stranger, on the 1,698th Day of the Drought, you were suddenly employed as a Third Level Guardian of the Central Core in the office of The Director of Finance. These facts are correct?"

"Yes, they are correct."

"Can you explain them to me?"

"Yes, I suppose so."

"Yes, I suppose so," she mocked me. "Well then, to what do you attribute your meteoric rise?"

"I applied for the job. I got the job."

The sarcasm in The Inquisitor's voice was scathing. "You simply walked into the Directorate, applied for a job and were given the job?"

"Yes."

"And Madame Director did not personally have anything to do with the decision?"

I was cautious. "No, no I do not think so."

The Inquisitor arched her eyebrows but, for whatever reason, my magic or otherwise, she accepted my answer. She stood and told me to take my clothes off, which I did. Then she came back around to the front of her desk. When she looked down at my enhanced member, she involuntarily moistened her upper lip. Then she again spread her legs, but she also ran her hand along her inner thigh up beneath her skirt. Her other hand reached inside her leather top and rested on her left breast.

"Madame Director is well known for liking special favors. It seems she again chose well."

I thought it was best to remain impassive, but my fear and The Inquisitor's provocative pose betrayed me. I tried to cross my legs to cover my arousal, but The Inquisitor was already focused on my erection. She left her desk, sat on the bench next to me, and proceeded to pleasure herself. She pulled her top down to her waist, laid across the bench on her back, pushed both her breasts together and told me to place my member between them.

I did as she told me to, and then I watched as I slid between The Inquisitor's two huge white breasts topped by erect nipples as large as the tips of my little fingers. As my arousal increased, The Inquisitor stretched her neck backwards between my legs so that her head rested on the floor. Because of her position, and because I was totally focused on the movement between her breasts, I could not see her cruel blue eyes or her twisted mouth. I was, therefore, totally unprepared for what happened next.

Just when my excitement was at its peak, and I was ready to release, I saw her breasts fall away from my member. Suddenly, I felt her fist wrap around me, and I assumed she was going to bring me to climax. Instead she held tightly to me, raised her head and bit my stones as hard as she could.

I cried out so loud I could not even hear myself. Shock waves coursed through my nerve endings. I sort of remember, even though my pain was so intense, that The Inquisitor's pleasure was so great as she watched me writhe on the bench, that I believe she actually reached climax at the very moment I passed out.

Anyway, however it happened, when I opened my eyes, I was flat on my back on the bench, and The Inquisitor was standing over me. My still engorged member remained clenched in her fist, and she had what I soon realized was a tattoo needle in her other hand. I watched through the painful fog enveloping my brain as The Inquisitor tattooed her name and a number on my flesh. When she was finished, she let go of me, and the pain was so excruciating I fainted again.

When I recovered consciousness, I was face down on the bench with my knees trussed up against my waist. Something cold and hard was being forced in and out of my body. I raised my head with some difficulty, and saw that a mirror had been placed in front of me, slightly off to one side so I could watch The Inquisitor pleasure herself while she violated me with her black 9mm pistol.

I tried to resist, to raise myself from the bench, but my pain was so great, I returned to the fetal position and let The Inquisitor have her way.

Her blue eyes burned with intense excitement. Her calf muscles tightened and she spread her legs slightly apart while her left hand played back and forth through her white curly hairs raising a flash of pink as she pulled her folds apart and moved her finger lightly across the head of her pearl. She thrust her pelvis forward and rocked on her heels which caused her huge breasts to bounce and roll. Her mouth opened slightly as she ran her tongue back and forth across her teeth. Her lips were contorted in a sneer. The muscles in her right arm were so tense I could see the veins pop along her biceps.

Then, without warning I began to cry. As my tears ran down my cheeks, I tried desperately to distract myself by focusing my attention on a chip in one of the tiles on the office floor. But the distraction did not really work. I assumed my life was over, and I more or less passively waited, in humiliation and resignation, for The Inquisitor to pull the trigger.

But she never did. The gun moved in and out with such fierce intensity it was easy to follow the rising path of The Inquisitor's excitement. I did not even have to look in the mirror. Finally she drove the pistol deep inside me all the way up to the trigger guard, and from the sounds of her grunting and groaning, I knew she had made herself climax again.

When her convulsions stopped, she laughed, sat down on the bench next to me and said: "I have tattooed my name, followed by the fact you were branded on the 1,734th Day of the Drought, onto your member. What do you think Madame Director will say about that?"

I tried to speak, but my voice was weak, rasping. "Why torture me if you really want her?"

"Because, dear Sandro, I want fear to permeate her organization, even the most insignificant parts of it. Change is in the wind. A new order will prevail, and I am going to destroy that bitch. She thinks she is.... Anyway, we have reports she is...is not exactly loyal."

"You want me to tell her what happened to me?"

"You will not have the chance, dear Sandro. You have helped her manipulate the markets. She has made enormous amounts of money which she does not share. Not with us anyway. You will simply disappear, and the photographic record of our little session will mysteriously be circulated throughout the Ministry."

Since I found it unlikely I could alter my fate, I spoke freely. "All of you in power say you fear the people, but in fact you fear each other... However, someday justice will rise from below and you will be destroyed because you are evil and the people will only tolerate evil for so long."

"Oh really?"

"There will be vengeance. There really will."

She laughed. "I find that is why you outlanders from the lower classes are so amusing. Simpletons. I really must find one of your young women to take as my next lover. She would be so, ah, so... romantic, yes, romantic. She might even believe she could save me. By the way, where did you get that fantastic member, dear Sandro?"

"Unlike you, I was born with one," I said. "Its size is to help me in my mission."

"And what, oh foolish stupid one, is this great mission?"

I looked her in the eye and said: "To rid this world of you and all those like you."

The Inquisitor tossed her head back and laughed so hard her breasts bounced up and down in rhythm with her chuckles. "I do so tremble at the thought you might try to rid the world of such as me," she said as she ran the barrel of her gun slowly up my spine. "Since you have such a wonderful sense of humor, I have decided I will spare your life."

She stood up, rearranged her top, pushed her skirt down onto her thighs and eased her pistol back into its holster. Then she went behind her desk and sat in her chair. "Are you not going to thank me?"

I felt no gratitude at all. In fact, at that moment I would have rather been dead. "May the Gods piss on your ugly white head," I said.

The Inquisitor was delighted. "Well, are we not feeling much better now, Sandro?"

"Yes, yes much better...," I said.

The Inquisitor clapped her hands. "So, since you are my friend, you do not have to remain here. I will let you go to live in a work camp."

"I would prefer death so my soul can raise an army of demons to clean out this place," I said.

The Inquisitor pressed a button on her desk and two guards entered her office.

"Superdump," said The Inquisitor, cryptically. Then she added, "On this, the 1,734th Day of the Drought, I, by the authority vested in me by the Central Administration, sentence this Outlander known as Sandro to reside at the Central Superdump until he is called to testify about certain matters of state security at an unspecified date in the future."

When The Inquisitor was finished speaking, the guards lifted me off of her bench and carried me away.

Chapter Seven: Chaos

Chaos is the normal state of existence.

The antidote to chaos is unity, a concept we impose so things appear to have the order, patterns and structures our brains use to create meaning. It is certainly true that without the concept of unity, without communion there is only loneliness, depression and despair. So, we reach out to each other. That reaching becomes a family; the family, a tribe; the tribe, a village; the village, a region; the region, a nation; and the nation, a state.

Then the state becomes oppressive. It regulates order without purpose. It chooses decisions which perpetuate its own existence. And then the people revolt. They reclaim their right to live their natural chaotic existence.

That is why revolutionaries become our most magnificent heroes, they reclaim our right to live in chaos. However, when chaos again brings loneliness, depression and despair, we burn the revolutionaries and bury their statues beneath the common refuse in isolated dumps.

Mariann and Alexander had become old statues, failed revolutionaries whose time had come and gone. They had been buried in the Superdump during their many years in exile and then forgotten.

Mariann was bent, worn and tired. Her hair was flecked with gray, her breasts hung loosely on her chest. Her green eyes had lost their luster, and her lids fluttered beneath her brow in nervous agitation. She never smiled. She never laughed. She never cried.

Alexander was tall, thin and gaunt. He had dull frightened eyes, bad teeth, a scraggly beard and a broken nose. His hair was thin and patchy, but mostly, he was bald.

Alexander shuffled from place to place with his head bowed toward the ground. He mumbled to himself. Sometimes he grew angry, and waved his hands and flailed his arms at the broiling empty sky. Mostly, he sat on the ground and traced patterns in the dirt.

They were both covered with the dust and the grit whipped about by the sweltering winds that blew across the dunes and valleys of the dump. They were scavengers who picked through the refuse of the perfect order they had once tried to overthrow for anything of value they could sell or barter for food and water.

I ran into them on the third day of my detention, when my body had healed a bit, and my hunger forced me to look for food.

I saw Mariann first. She was pulling rusted metal rods off a pile and sorting them by length. Her movements were repetitious and resigned. The sorted pile grew very slowly.

As I approached her, I saw Alexander on the other side of the pile, tracing a dirt painting with a long bent stick. His strokes were tentative and lackadaisical; his art uninspired. Mariann and Alexander were both clearly marking time.

Alexander was actually the first one to see me, so I walked over to him. But he continued to move his stick about in the dirt and pretended he had not seen me.

I said, "I need help."

I did not notice her at first, but Mariann had approached me from behind. When I turned around, she held one of her metal rods in her hands as if it were a weapon. "Leave him alone," she said. "He will not harm you...in fact, leave us both alone."

"But I am hungry," I said.

"We have nothing," said Mariann.

I felt weak so I sat on top of a discarded wooden crate. The winds were blowing fiercely, and all three of us were trying to shield our faces from the heat, the glare and the soot.

"Look," I said, "I do not mean to bother, but I have been dropped here by the security police, and I do not know how...I do not know...how to survive. I need help."

"Who dropped you here?" Alexander asked.

I told them a little bit about The Inquisitor although I thought it best to leave out the events which had gotten me into trouble in the first place.

My mention of The Inquisitor seemed to perk Mariann and Alexander's interest. "Welcome to the village of the damned," said Alexander. He tapped his stick against my leg. "Plan for a long stay, young fellow."

"What in the world did you do?" asked Mariann.

"I was out before curfew ended...with no papers."

Mariann and Alexander reverted to their earlier caution. "They do not send curfew violators here," said Alexander.

"You are a spy," said Mariann. "Leave us alone. We have suffered enough."

I stood up and started to walk away. "Wait a minute," Alexander called after me. He turned to Mariann. "A spy would come up with a better story than that."

"Just let him go," she whispered.

I continued to walk away from them when I heard Alexander shuffle up behind me. I turned around so quickly I accidentally startled Alexander who raised his stick into the air.

"Are you a spy?" Alexander asked. "Please tell me the truth, are you a spy."

"No," I said.

Alexander lowered his stick. "Then come back to us," he

pleaded. "We are lonely, and we have had no one to talk to for a long time."

I returned to my crate and sat silently. Finally, Alexander asked me who I really was. I told them my story, slowly at first, then the words came rushing out of me. When I finished, I was both relieved and exhausted.

I did notice that Alexander and Mariann had become more interested as my story progressed. I saw them exchange glances and nod toward each other at certain points. As I sat there with my head in my hands I could not understand why they both stared at me with something approaching awe. Mariann, in particular, could not contain her curiosity. "Do you know the meaning of what you have just told us?" she asked.

"My story has no meaning at all," I said. "That is the problem. I feel like all these things have happened to me which... which do not really have any meaning."

"Maybe La Bruja gave you a dream potion." Alexander said. He turned to Mariann. "I think he is hallucinating."

"What I have told you is what happened," I said.

"Do you still seek vengeance?" asked Mariann.

"Yes, of course," I said, but there was doubt in my voice. Even I could not help but notice it. "At least I think I do." Then I thought about Mariann's question a little more. "But I am also...well...I am not certain about anything anymore. I would like to see the rulers pay for their crimes, but I am very tired and I do not think I can do much. Sometimes I just wish I could go home. Sometimes..."

"If your story is true," said Mariann, "you could not possibly understand it. You are involved in something much, much bigger than you can imagine. You may be..."

"Yes, he may be the one," said Alexander.

"He could be," said Mariann.

I asked them what they meant, but they would not answer

me. Instead they offered me food. They gave me a little water to drink. They asked me a few more questions. They continued to stare at me, and they whispered to each other from time to time.

Finally they seemed to reach some sort of consensus. "What day is it?" Alexander asked.

I told them I was pretty sure it was the 1,735th Day of the Drought. "Ah, well yes, then of course," said Mariann without really explaining.

And that was how my training began.

Mariann and Alexander taught me everything about The First Drought and The Famine that followed it. They explained how the Central Authorities had crushed the revolt that stemmed from that famine. They told me what they had done to promote the first great uprising and why. They told me of their own capture and torture by The Inquisitor, and how they had learned to survive in the Superdump.

I did not know whether to believe most of what they told me because I had already become suspicious of everybody. But Mariann and Alexander's stories helped pass the endlessly boring, repetitious, hot, sunny days. And, whether the stories affected me in the way they were intended to or not, their telling had a profound effect on the storytellers themselves.

Mariann's eyes picked up a twinkle. Her gaze was tough and steady. The gray in her hair looked more like highlights streaked into her natural color. She held her back straight so her breasts stood higher and more firmly when she walked.

As the days passed, she took to weaving brightly colored rags braided into her hair. She fashioned metal bracelets from scrap. She made rings from tin and pieces of broken glass. She was clean. She was orderly. She was animated.

She laughed a lot. She smiled, and she cried.

Alexander's transformation was, if anything, even more

dramatic. He stood tall and erect, and walked about with a jaunty air. His clothes were neat and fresh. He wore a torn but still elegant straw hat he discovered among the ruins, pulled down over his eyes at a rakish angle.

His mind was sharp and alert. He spoke in a clear, articulate voice filled with hope and passion.

Together they began to call me The Chosen One; and, despite my requests to stop doing so, they refused to call me by any other name.

One night, when a full moon rose over the dry riverbed that ran alongside the dump, and the setting sun painted a rose and purple sky behind the ragged hills of garbage, Mariann began to tell the story of the Cactus Hill rebellion, the mythic event which liberated Central City for three days before it was retaken by the Central Authorities. Mariann and Alexander had been the revolutionary co-mayors during that liberation.

As Mariann's storytelling became more excited and energetic, her loose-fitting clothes began to come undone, and her breasts, stomach and hips were often exposed. I found myself staring at her naked flesh and becoming excited. Mariann noticed my attention and stopped in the middle of her recitation. She looked at me quizzically, unable to believe her body really interested me. Then when she was convinced I really was watching her, she turned her back, unbuttoned her dress and let it slip to the ground. Then she turned around and faced Alexander and me.

There was a flicker of fear in her eyes while she waited for our disgust or disapproval, but neither of us felt either of those emotions. Alexander beamed. I smiled.

Mariann stopped talking and began to dance in the moonlight. As she danced her body transformed itself. Her buttocks and thighs were tight and muscled. Her nipples were extended and the moonlight glistened against the tiny beads of sweat on the protruding tips of her breasts.

Then Alexander stood up and pulled his pants down. His member, which had not been erect for many years, that night stood long and hard and true. He took off his shirt and raised his hands in the air. He snapped his fingers three times, and then joined Mariann in the dance.

They instinctively formed a perfectly complimentary choreography, gleaned from many years of following each other's movements. They moved together and touched each other, then moved apart. Their touching became slower, more intimate and sensual. Alexander cupped Mariann's breasts with his hands. She stroked his member. He kissed her neck. She fondled his bottom. He ran his tongue across her stomach. She scratched his back. He lifted her hair and licked the back of her neck. She pinched his thighs. And still they danced.

I watched their passionate reverie with growing arousal. They were so slow and patient, so careful and yet casual, precise and knowing. When they looked into each other's eyes, lifetimes shot across the space between them and brought them together. When they were excited, their sighs and moans ached with a tremulous intensity. They were wonderful.

After a while, their dancing slowed. They held on to each other more, and they separated less often. Finally they danced toward me totally wrapped around each other. They stopped in front of me and Mariann fell to the ground in front of Alexander. Her eyes were wide and her hands actually shook as she reached out for his member and took it into her mouth. When she began her gentle worship, Alexander reared back his head and let out an enormous cry. Then he stood on his toes, held her head in his hands and moved himself in and out of Mariann's mouth.

Mariann took one hand from Alexander's member and used it to caress his bottom. With her other hand she reached out to me.

I took her hand and moved over to them. Mariann motioned for me to get behind her, which I did. Then she presented herself to my throbbing flesh. When I pressed myself up into the gateway between her legs, I was delighted to find her tight and more moist than I would have assumed. I immediately started to move within her with a rhythm that was both hard and deep, while she continued worshipping Alexander.

Alexander stopped speaking about revolution, and began to chant in unknown languages about unknowable things. He danced lightly on his toes in rhythm with Mariann's movements. He raised his arms toward the moon. His hands called forth the night spirits of chaos. The white moonlight emphasized the veins along his forehead which bulged and pulsed as did the veins in his member.

The three of us continued to flow into one another through Mariann's body. She was lost in total ecstasy. Her flesh again became the complete and perfect instrument of her desire. I put my hands on her bottom and squeezed her flesh so hard I could feel her bones underneath the skin.

At that very moment, Mariann gave up on any remaining control in favor of a totally abandoned passion. The ribbons in her hair became a kaleidoscope of color as she shook her head in the moonlight. Her bottom bounced up and down in ecstatic spasms.

Alexander, who believed he would never have such an experience again, continued to speak in tongues. Then he let out one last cry and released himself all over Mariann's face and into her hair ribbons. I realized they had made me so aroused I was ready to release, so I withdrew, and let my seed fly over Mariann's bony, moving bottom.

Mariann went wild. She started crying out, "He is the one;

good lord, almighty he really is the one." Then, "I have been consecrated; on this, the 1,756th Day of the Drought, I have been blessed; before the end, I have finally come to feel the light!"

Meanwhile Alexander was chanting at the top of his lungs in yet another strange, guttural language. Both of them were dancing and howling and carrying on and in general making an awful racket when we heard the first shots from behind one of the larger garbage dunes.

A lifetime of experience made Mariann and Alexander immediately plunge toward the ground, face down in the dirt. When the shots continued and raised little puffs of dirt near me, I joined them.

"It is the Authorities," whispered Alexander.

"We have got to save The Chosen One," said Mariann.

"The moonlight is a problem," said Alexander. More shots rang out. The bullets landed very close to us.

"I guess this is it," said Mariann. She reached out, held Alexander's hand and squeezed it. "I love you," she said to him.

Alexander spoke to me: "When we run, you must roll away and get behind that hillock off to our left. Then you need to head for the tunnels down by the riverbed. The fourth tunnel is unknown to them. Remember to pull the cover over the entrance. And..."

"No," I said. "I will not leave without you."

"Yes you will," said Mariann. "You must. You are The Chosen One, the hope of a future for the people."

"What is this 'Chosen One' nonsense?" I said angrily.

"You will learn soon enough," said Alexander as he placed his arm on my shoulder.

More shots rang out. From the sounds of the firing, it was clear the guards were getting closer.

"We have given you the beginnings of your story," said

Mariann. "Now you must live the rest of it." A bullet landed near her leg. She kissed me on the lips. "Our time is coming to an end. We must go to another place."

Alexander gave me one last embrace. "Remember us," he said. "But do not be sad. We are happy. We could not have wished for a better way…"

Then before I could stop them they both leapt to their feet and took off in the opposite direction from where they had told me to escape.

To this day I remember hearing the bullets' dull thuds as they pounded into Alexander and Mariann's flesh, but I refused to look. I ran in the opposite direction and slipped behind the hill on the left just as the guards approached the lifeless forms sprawled on the ground. In their frustration, they pumped a few more bullets into the bodies and kicked and slammed them with their rifle butts, but Mariann and Alexander did not feel the pain. Their spirits had soared into the light.

I did make it to the fourth tunnel. I pulled the cover over me as I descended beneath the Superdump. I placed my right hand on the side of the tunnel and followed it wherever it led me. After some time I saw the white moonlight ahead of me, and I picked up my pace as I ran for the exit.

The tunnel emptied into the dry riverbed about three hundred meters past the dump itself. I could barely hear the guards who were still shouting, but I clearly did hear the sounds of a flying gunboat approaching the riverbed. I crouched as low as I was able and kept running. I ran as fast as I could for as long as I could, and then when I realized I was free, I collapsed onto the soft sand of the Great Desert.

Rain

Chapter Eight: Life

ll the earth is bursting with life.

In the forests, the animals and insects and flowers and trees are obvious and overwhelming. The oceans teem with fish and mammals and plants and crustaceans. Even the barren northern tundra is not truly barren, but fertile ground for lichens and ferrets and big-horned mammals.

But all those places have one thing in common: they all have water. Water falling from the sky in pounding floods or caressing the earth in soft, gentle mists; water cascading down jagged mountain cliffs; water rolling through the countryside in giant muddy rivers; water from the melting snow and ice of prehistoric glaciers; water forcing its way up through the ground in fresh, cold springs; water spewing into the air from boiling geysers; water floating on the air in a dense, gray fog.

Of course, there did not seem to be any water on the Great Desert; and at first, I did not believe there was any life. But it was there. There were tiny delicate flowers that stored up every trace of moisture until they suddenly bloomed in dazzling pinks and golds and mauves and magentas. There were lizards and snakes and scorpions which burrowed deep into the earth and found microscopic traces of condensation. There were tall stately cacti and short, squat tumbleweeds.

There were people, too, for the Great Desert was home to the Shadowless Ones, former revolutionaries, their families, their children and their grandchildren who fled into the wastelands in desperate exile. After a time, they stayed not only to avoid the Central Authorities, but because they had come to prefer the dangerous, lonely, silent freedom of the desert.

They were called shadowless because they taught themselves to blend into the sand and rocks and cliffs and hills. I certainly never knew they were anywhere near me until they chose to make themselves known.

They did so choose in the late afternoon, the day after my escape from the prison camp at the Superdump.

Although I had managed to get away from the dump, my predicament had hardly improved. I was alone on an enormous desert, unprotected, without food or water. In the early morning, I had, of course, been elated, hopeful, full of strength and resolve. But by late morning, I was already dehydrated, frightened and confused. By that afternoon I was beginning to envy Mariann and Alexander their quick, relatively painless death: I was delirious, badly burned and resigned to my own slow agonizing fate when I found a small sandstone outcropping and crawled under the rocks to await the inevitable.

The next thing I remember was looking into the wide eyes of a child whose tiny hands were pressed against my forehead. I assume it must have been my awakening that startled her because she withdrew her hands and skittered out from under the rocks onto the open desert, her brown cloak and bent stature immediately providing invisibility.

I tried to call after her, but when I opened my mouth, all that came out was a very hoarse whisper. As things turned out, it did not matter because within a few minutes, dusty brown forms of all shapes and sizes were gathered around me. One hand gave me a very small drink of water. Another pressed a damp cloth against my face. A third rubbed a soothing balm over my body.

Then they lifted me onto a stretcher, threw one of their cloaks over me and whisked me off to their encampment.

The silent procession arrived at the camp just as the sun was setting. More shapeless forms came out to greet us. People embraced and touched foreheads, but there was none of the laughter or shouting I would have expected to hear at such a homecoming. Most communication took place through hand signals and meaningful glances.

As evening approached, no fires were lit and no lights came on, but darkness did not bother the Shadowless Ones who seemed to relish it and, in fact, to grow in number as the light disappeared. Their energy and their activities also increased as the dusk turned to total darkness. What to me were barely distinguishable forms passing in the twilight, were to those people the commerce of their tribe. Families gathered for dinner, children played, adolescents courted, adults traded and bartered.

Eventually I was moved inside a cave where it was completely dark. I could not even see my hands in front of my face, although I did sense movement when the forms who had brought me inside then shuffled away. After they left, both the darkness and the silence were complete.

I lay there in the cave and tried to be brave, but the complete lack of sensory stimulation was terrifying. I thought of the fortune teller who had first set me on this path. I wondered about Maria and whether she had truly betrayed me or saved me. I remembered The Inquisitor's cruelty and shuddered. The darkness pressed against me like a living thing.

Then I felt the air move and heard a voice full of music and laughter and song say: "Welcome to our place, Sandro."

I tried to see someone, anyone, but I could see absolutely nothing. I reached out into the emptiness around me with my hands outstretched as far as I could stretch them, but I touched nothing, no one. "How do you know my name?" I asked.

The beautiful voice chose not to answer. Instead it said: "Sandro, I am sorry for the darkness, but we have learned to live mostly at night, without light. We communicate mostly through silent speaking. These things are helpful. They protect us."

"But you speak," I said, "and you not only speak, your voice is...beautiful. Who are you?"

"I am the Voice of the Shadowless Ones," it said. What felt like a hand brushed against my cheek, but when I reached out, I felt nothing. Then I smelled a sharp, unpleasant odor much like sour milk. "Drink this," the voice said. "You will sleep."

I felt the cup in my hands, and, because it was that extraordinary voice telling me to do so, I ignored my fears and drank.

I do not know how long I slept, but when I awoke I was again outside at dusk, and the activities going on around me were as they were the evening before.

After certain Shadowless Ones had cleaned and fed me, I was moved back into the cave. Although my body felt much better, I still found it frightening to lay there in total darkness. Painful memories haunted me. I thought of my fortune teller's prophecy. I tried yet again to figure out why Maria had thrown me out. I cringed when I remembered The Inquisitor, and I cried when I thought of Mariann and Alexander's courage and sacrifice. I was trembling when the voice returned.

"We must talk, Sandro," the voice said. "But first...it is our custom to please those we find on the desert. How can we please you?"

"Let me have light. Let me see you."

"That Sandro, I cannot do."

Then I said: "For those of us who live in the light, complete darkness is terrifying. For me," I said, "it is especially painful."

"What are you afraid of?"

"The memories..." I could barely speak. "...that I will touch something that will...that will make me feel bad."

"Then I will give you the opposite. You will not touch or be touched, yet you will have great pleasure."

The voice began to sing. The first notes were of such clarity, such power and force, they resonated through the bones in my head and stimulated the sensual zones of my brain. The next few notes were soft lips gently kissing my dry, parched mouth. Then there was a rest filled with expectations. Then a run which touched me like the tip of a wet tongue sliding down my neck to my chest. Another rest. Then, oh yes, throat singing in a minor key sent shivers all over my back. The final notes of that first chorus were perfumed gentle breezes blowing across my naked body.

I closed my eyes and let the music take hold of me. I floated away on soft billowing clouds to the southern rain forests and landed in a glade canopied by giant trees with thick flower-covered vines hanging from the upper branches. Luxuriant ferns taller than palm trees filtered whatever sunlight was not blocked by the trees. I rested on a carpet of thick, green moss. Blue and red and green birds with orange and black beaks perched in the vines preening themselves.

Then the voice sang a banquet of exotic fruits, spicy meats, tart herbs and wet vegetables, sparkling drinks and rich, ripe sweets served by beautiful young men and women clothed only in transparent gowns of diaphanous silk. They kissed me and caressed me as each new taste lingered on my lips. They licked my toes and touched my fingers as each new smell tickled my nose. They offered me their members and nipples to worship as each new morsel slid down my throat, slowly...sensually.

Then the voice laughed, giggled and sighed. It moaned a little, laughed again and then whispered. It coaxed, it teased, it promised, it withdrew. The voice sang music that trickled down from my brain to my heart. It sat, curled inside my chest, it rumbled and shook in time with the blood coursing through my veins. That music, that wonderful sweet music...

My body responded to the auditory touch. My member grew. My nipples were hard. I ran my tongue along my lips. My body tightened and my stomach rippled. I rolled my shoulders in their sockets. My fingers stretched and curled. My hips swiveled. My member grew even larger as I pushed it up into the darkness, and my breathing mimicked the rhythms of my blood and the music, that wonderful sweet music...

Then the voice became a thousand fingernails each lightly scratching my scalp, my neck, my chest, my back, my hips, my thighs, my knees, my calves, my feet and each of my toes, tickling slowly and suggestively across the webbing and then up and down each toe. The voice became a thousand wet little tongues moving inside my ears, against my skin, along the tip of my member. And still it pulled me higher...ever higher...

Finally the music rose to a crescendo of ecstasy, a tight, wet, moist opening that squeezed against my member and pulled, released, pulled, released, faster and higher and higher. And the more the voice rose, the more my body trembled and shook, and I was pulled and released even faster, and I was carried...even...higher, pulled and released...faster...higher...

And then the voice which had brought me to the edge dropped suddenly to a lower register where it began to moan and whimper, and I released in a fountain I could not see, but I could feel my seed land on my stomach and thighs.

Then the voice was soft and comforting until my normal breathing returned. After a few moments rest, the voice said: "Are you still afraid, Sandro?"

"No," I said. "I am not afraid."

"Then we can begin," said the voice. "Do you know who you are?"

"Of course," I said, slightly annoyed, "I have been me all my life."

"Well said," the voice responded. Then there was musical laughter. "A good joke, Sandro. But do you know who you really are?"

"Apparently not," I said. "It seems everyone else has a plan for me. They take me places and tell me what to do. They treat me with respect or scorn or worse, but I never really understand what they are talking about."

"Why do you not believe them?"

I explained that first of all, I sought, if anything, only revenge, not fame or glory. Furthermore, I told the voice, it was not my nature to take seriously assertions that anyone was particularly special or unique. I argued that all people were, after all, pretty simple, they ate, they slept, they joined, they died.

There was more lilting laughter. Then a sound of amusement as the voice responded. "You are of course right, Sandro. That is all there is to a life. But what is there to the living of a life? What are the textures, the colors, the scents of a life? We grow sensitive to those things here on the desert."

"I have also grown more sensitive in this darkness."

"That is true, you have, and it is important that your sensitivity continue to grow. But tell me, Sandro, what do you know of your own history? Of where you came from before Central City?"

I thought about this. "Very little. I was born in the coastal villages. My parents died when I was young. I came to Central City seeking work."

"And what brought your parents to the coast?"

"I do not know. I never asked."

"Your grandmother was from the hill tribes," said the voice. "Your grandfather was a merchant who traveled the old trade routes. In your blood runs the heritage of wanderers and rebels, of those who crossed deserts and mountains, of those who refused to submit to any authority but their own conscience."

"How do you know this?"

"We know many things in the darkness, Sandro. We read the signs that others miss. We see what the light blinds people to. Your body carries marks, not just the tattoo The Inquisitor placed on you, but older marks. The talisman around your neck hums with La Bruja's magic. Your enhanced member is not natural, yet it has become part of you. These things tell us you are being prepared for something."

"Prepared by whom?"

"By forces older than the Central Authorities. By the shadow world that La Bruja showed you. By the spirits that Mariann and Alexander called forth in their final dance. By the same power that has kept this desert alive despite centuries without rain."

I was silent, processing this.

"And there is something else," the voice continued. "Something you have not yet understood about yourself. You have been marked by water, Sandro. When you were a child, did you nearly drown?"

I felt a chill. "Yes. How did you know?"

"Because those who are chosen to bring the rain must first be claimed by water. It is an old law, older than memory. You died in that water, Sandro, and you were reborn. That is when you became The Chosen One, though you did not know it yet."

"I do not remember dying."

"The body remembers what the mind forgets. That is why you fear the darkness, it reminds you of being underwater, of drowning. But it is also why you can survive what would kill others. You have already died once. A second death holds no power over you."

The voice paused, and I heard something like a smile in its next words. "And so, you shall stay in the darkness for two more days. I will caress you and make love to you without touching you. I will heal your mind and spirit. But after two days, you must leave this cave. On the third day, you will leave the Great Desert, recross the dry riverbed and reenter the city."

"That will be suicide."

"No, Sandro, because you really are The Chosen One. The talisman will protect you. Your magic will shield you. And the people are waiting, though they do not yet know it."

The voice said that with such finality, I did not argue. The darkness became a warm clear liquid that wrapped around me and gave me strength. The voice sang a lullaby, and I dissolved into a deep, deep sleep.

The voice did as it said it would, and I used that time alone in the darkness to contemplate what was happening to me.

Over those two days, the voice sang to me of ancient histories and future prophecies. It told me of the first rains that created the world, and the last rains that would wash away the corrupt order. It sang of heroes who had tried and failed, of martyrs who gave their lives for freedom, of ordinary people who became extraordinary when the moment demanded it.

And it pleasured me again and again, each time differently, each time teaching my body to respond to sound and air and imagination rather than touch. By the third day, I had learned to find ecstasy in the absence of contact, to feel presence in emptiness, to see light in darkness.

The truth is I began to seriously consider that perhaps I was special in some way, that I really was The Chosen One, that in fact I, Sandro, who had never done anything of any real value in my entire life, could bring rain and set the people free.

And then, three days later, on the 1,761st Day of the Drought, I followed instructions, left the Great Desert, and returned to Central City.

Rain

Chapter Nine: Laws

Laws are the rules by which we play our games. We assume if we play by the rules, we will always be allowed to participate whether we win or not. In fact, playing by the rules often keeps us out of the game; or perhaps the games we think we are playing are not the actual games being played. Either way, it is often wise to break the law if we want something.

Of course, breaking the law leaves us flying through the air with no safety net. If we do not perform the trick perfectly, we die.

And, after leaving the desert, I was tired of flirting with death. I was tired of being alone and an outcast. If I was going to be able to complete my mysterious mission, I wanted friends, people I could talk to and relax with. I wanted to feel I was not being hunted all the time.

But I had made my decision when I cast my lot with Maria, and I was a renegade whether I liked it or not. I was an outlaw with a bounty on my head and a strange destiny I did not understand.

Actually when I returned from the Great Desert, I thought I would be picked up immediately by The Inquisitor's Searchers, but, to my amazement, I penetrated all the way to the inner core of Central City, and no one challenged me or questioned me. However, when dawn broke the following day, I decided not to push my luck, and I began to search for a hiding place.

I found myself in a section of the city where there were many old, abandoned warehouses. Their rusted roofs, broken windows and burned out shells were interspersed among newer, concrete structures. I first tried to find an open gate so I could slip into one of the empty yards and hide among the weather-beaten crates and bins. But all the gates were locked, or they were guarded by uniformed thugs with attack dogs. Then I found an open door that led into one of the newer complexes. I found an unoccupied guardhouse where there was a small stock of tinned food. After I ate one tin of fruit, I crawled off between two large metal boxes filled with electronic equipment and went to sleep.

I was awakened a few hours later by two dogs who were growling and barking viciously somewhere near where I was sleeping. I opened my eyes fully expecting to see their bared teeth and dripping saliva, but it turned out the dogs were not upset by my presence. They were reacting to the gang of underclass revolutionaries streaming in through the same open door I had discovered hours earlier.

Within minutes, the gang had complete control of the warehouse. The dogs were dead, and a frightened security guard was bound and gagged in a corner of the building. At that point, the raiders spread throughout the building, carefully picking and choosing those communication components they had obviously selected beforehand.

It did not take long before they also found me. They forced me to kneel on the floor while they tied my hands and feet. Then they dragged me over to the corner where the guard was whimpering and shaking, and they dumped me there while they went about their work.

When they returned to deal with the guard and me, they first removed the gag from the guard's mouth and questioned him about certain pieces of equipment and where they were stored. The poor guard was so frightened he could barely speak. Once they became convinced he was no longer of any value to them, they killed him.

Then they questioned me. Despite my protests that I knew nothing, that I myself was part of the underground and that I was only hiding in the warehouse until I could find a better place, they were inclined to kill me too. Then the leader of the gang said, "perhaps we should wait for Doebuck."

The members of the gang were arguing about their choices when Doebuck entered the warehouse. The gangsters immediately stepped aside in deference to their chief.

Doebuck was a titan...a, well, he was astonishing. He was very tall, taller than any other member of the gang. His skin was very dark, so black he would have been invisible in the dark tunnels and unlit sewers where the gang lived had it not been for his long, straight, bleached-blond hair that ran half way down his back.

He wore a red and yellow silk headband, and no clothes other than a red leather thong which in back was stretched against his body, and in front formed a sheath that covered a magnificent organ almost 30cm long, 4cm thick at the base, 2.5cm at the tip.

But Doebuck's startling appearance did not end with his height and his member. He was also a hermaphrodite, his full breasts and large nipples were prominent and well-formed, the perfect work of the renegade underground surgeon, the infamous white-haired tiny, demented Dr. Reginald Pritowski who accompanied Doebuck everywhere and joined in Doebuck's reveries.

Despite my fear, I was just coming to terms with the image of Doebuck when I realized the apparition approaching me held a long black leather leash which was attached to a spiked dog collar which was, in turn, wrapped around the neck of a pale, subservient woman who trailed behind him. When I saw the woman's face, my heart skipped a beat and I blurted out, in spite of myself, "Oh my!"

The Publisher did not react to my cry. She stared straight ahead, but Doebuck pulled on her leash and brought her around in front of me. "Do you know this pig?" Doebuck asked her.

"I thought she was someone else," I said quickly.

The Publisher's voice was flat, hollow. "I do not know him."

"Do you?" Doebuck was yelling. "Do you expect me to believe that?" He not only refused to believe her, he reached out his hand toward one of the gang members who handed him a sharp, glistening sword. Then Doebuck took the sword, raised it in the air and stepped closer to me.

"No," I said. Suddenly, I remembered my tattoo. "Look," I said as I held out my own rather impressive organ for Doebuck to see.

Doebuck stopped his advance and lowered his sword. "Hmm," he said with some curiosity, "not bad. Not nearly so large as mine though." He reached down and undid his thong and removed the sheath from his member. "Look at this one!"

"I did not wish to compare mine with your own most splendid organ," I said. "I only wanted to show you The Inquisitor's mark." I cradled my member in my hand and displayed my tattoo. "I would not have this tattoo if I were on the side of the Central Authorities."

"Doc," said Doebuck to Pritowski, "examine this, and tell me if it is real."

Pritowski propped his eyeglasses on his forehead, took my member in his hand and squinted as he ran his finger along the numbers. "I cannot tell," he mumbled.

"Run your finger along it a little more, and it will be large enough to see," I said.

Pritowski liked that idea, and, as he rubbed, my member grew. Pritowski stood up and lowered his glasses again. "Looks real to me," he finally said.

But Doebuck again raised his sword, and I closed my eyes, waiting for him to strike. I did hear the sword rush through the air, then I felt the rope around my feet fall away. I opened my eyes and saw that the sword had sliced cleanly through the rope. Then Doebuck moved behind me, and with one more slice released my hands.

"For the moment, I will allow you to live," said Doebuck. "As for the future, well...we shall see."

At that point another member of the gang rushed into the room and spoke to Doebuck: "It is time. Our Insiders have sent us messages that the authorities are close, very close."

Doebuck signaled the other members of his gang, "Take care of it, then." He looked at me. "You must come with us."

"Yes," I said.

Someone placed a hood over my head. One of the gangsters took my hand and whispered, in a heavy outland accent, "Follow me in complete trust and without hesitation. Otherwise, you will die."

The group moved out of the warehouse into the hot morning air, across some sticky pavement, then down through a hole into a damp smelly area. A few seconds after I heard a clanking metal sound above my head, I also heard a tremendous explosion which rocked the walls of our underground escape route. I assumed that blast meant the end of the communications warehouse.

Then the group, led by Doebuck, wandered through a series of tunnels and sewers for what seemed to me like hours. We were always heading down, deeper into the earth. As we descended, the air grew cooler, then hotter. Sweat poured down my face and under my hood. I felt like I was going to collapse when suddenly everyone stopped. Although it was no cooler where we were, the air was less tight and dank. A series of drafts blew across my body, and I knew we were inside a larger area, perhaps a large cavern. I smelled smoke and realized there were probably fires all around me. Then I heard cheers and laughter, and I knew we had arrived at the gang's home base.

I was told to sit down. I did, and then I was left hooded and ignored for an hour or so. I heard sighs and moans and groans amidst the laughter and occasional cheering, but I had no real idea of what was actually going on.

Eventually my hood was removed, and the very first scene I saw was The Publisher and Doebuck backlit by a roaring bonfire. The Publisher was sucking on Doebuck's left breast while his huge member plunged in and out of her. Sweat poured down both of their bodies as the flames leapt higher and Doebuck's great strength pushed The Publisher to her limits.

When Doebuck was finished, he tied The Publisher's leash to a thick wooden pole and sauntered over to speak to me.

"She never gets enough," said Doebuck. I kept my mouth shut and said nothing. Doebuck continued: "We found her wandering in an alley during one of our raids. She was mumbling something about being attacked by The Inquisitor's guards and she barely escaped. Do you know anything about that?"

"No," I said, "but I can guess what happened."

I reminded Doebuck that there were constant power struggles going on within the inner circle of the Central Authorities. Then I added, "I think your slave, who was The Publisher of The Central Authoritarian, was planning some sort of coup which was foiled by The Inquisitor."

"How would you know that?" Doebuck asked.

"Because...because there were rumors everywhere just before

I went under torture by The Inquisitor at the Central Station," I said. Then I told Doebuck more of my story. When I finished, Doebuck's attitude toward me seemed to change.

"And there are those who have actually been calling you 'The Chosen One'?"

"Yes," I said.

"And they say you will lead The Great Overthrow?"

"No, no one has said that. I do not know what that means."

Doebuck did not respond. He was lost in his own thoughts for a while, then he said: "If you have lived through these things, and if you are The Chosen One, how can you not know about The Great Overthrow?"

I offered the only explanation available to me: "I did not say I am The Chosen One. I have only said that others have called me that."

"They are wrong," said Doebuck. "You are not The Chosen One. I am certain of that." Again he considered his thoughts. "For one thing, although I admit your member is very large, mine is bigger."

"That is true," I said.

Doebuck rose and placed a chain link choke collar around my neck. Then he attached a longer chain to the collar, pulled me over to the pole where The Publisher was tethered and secured me to the same pole. Then Doebuck untied The Publisher, threw her to the ground, thrust his gargantuan organ into her, placed his arms beneath her bottom, raised her into the air and took her with incredible ferocity.

And they were not alone. Off to their right was a huge blond with the largest breasts I had ever seen. She was kneeling on all fours, her breasts nearly brushing against the ground while the mad old Doctor Pritowski took her from behind with his small member. The doctor's glasses bounced on his enormous nose as he screamed and shouted, "Mama, Mama, your little boy...your little Priti will make everything all right...Mama, Mama oh, oh, oh, my Mama..." at which point the blond moved her hips, shook her breasts and extended her tongue into the air.

To their left, two women danced together. The older, dark-haired one had her eyes closed and her head arched back so that the younger curly-haired one with the pear shaped bottom could kiss the woman's neck and lick her chest and squeeze the older woman's dark brown nipples between her nimble young fingers. The older woman had one hand inside the younger girl's opening and her other hand caressed the girl's soft, smooth bottom. As I turned away, the younger one had the older woman's peaks between her teeth and was biting them so hard the older woman cried out.

Behind them I could just manage to catch the outlines of two young boys kissing while they stroked each other's members. One was a peaches and cream blond; the other a freckle-faced red head. An older man knelt behind the blond boy and kissed the young man while he furiously stroked his own withered member with his left hand.

Below the rock where Doebuck and The Publisher were joined, a malformed dwarf was furiously whipping a stunning brunette whose dress was hiked up over her buttocks so she could bare her bottom to the whip's sting. The dwarf actually leapt off the ground as he brought the leather strips back behind his head and then down with all his strength. Mascara-stained tears flowed from the brunette's eyes and stained her mouth and neck. She licked the salty black drops with a long pink tongue that rotated round and round her thick, fleshy lips.

Then I noticed that right behind me was a man with slanted eyes, golden skin, and jet black, long, straight hair who was sliding his slippery moist member into a dark skinned beauty whose opening was still quivering and wet from her adventures with an extremely unattractive, pock-faced, sallow-skinned man whose body, bulging biceps, thickly muscled thighs, washboard stomach and highly defined pectorals, more than compensated for his looks. He watched the long-haired man with the golden skin as if he was studying the man's technique, and he probably was.

Then a raucous horn resounded from somewhere further inside the cavern. The sound reverberated deep in the pit of my stomach, bounced off the walls and washed across me again just in time for the next blast to come rolling into the room. The effect was hypnotic; and as the notes continued, all the bodies swayed and jerked and moved and stroked in rhythm, and their forms shimmied and danced against the smoke and fires so that the outlaw gang itself became one living organism in its moving and touching and dancing and joining and licking and kissing and sighing and laughing and crying.

And then, the gang was one in its climax. In its grand, ecstatic, wonderful climax when the huge blond with the large breasts screamed and the mad Doctor Pritowski released himself all over her bottom, and when the dark haired older woman shuddered, when the younger curly haired girl with the pear shaped bottom shook, and the two boys cried out as they covered each other, and the old man fell back in convulsions, and the dwarf pushed the whip handle into the brunette's soaking opening and she spread apart her bottom so that he could blow his hot breath across her tight entrance, and the long-haired man released inside the dark skinned beauty, and the muscled warrior exploded in yet another climax, and above them all Doebuck's incredible organ let loose a thunderstorm of white rain which covered The Publisher from her long light brown hair down to her curled little toes.

Then, just as my own excitement began to stir up inside me, the trumpet stopped. There was complete silence while the brass echoes faded away. Then the different groupings coiled around each other and went to sleep. The flames died down, and in the smoky half-light I tried to bring myself to climax. I was almost ready to release when I became aware that The Publisher, who had remained untied once Doebuck was finished with her, was watching me. She made certain Doebuck was sleeping, then she crawled over, and without asking, took my member and drew on it until I released in her mouth.

When I was finished, she whispered in my ear, "Of course I remember you. You were the one who disciplined me and brought me to Maria."

I grabbed hold of The Publisher's arms. "Where is Maria? What happened to her?"

"I am not certain," said The Publisher, "So much has happened since then. I heard she has been sent to the camps, others have told me she is in the Central Penitentiary, but I believe she is still free.

"Look, Sandro, I am sorry we threw you out, but I needed Maria to complete my plan. Unfortunately it was not a very good plan.

"We were ambushed, you know. We thought The Director of Finance was on our side, but she betrayed us to The Inquisitor in order to save her own skin...However, we do not have much time to talk. You must know you are in great, great danger here."

"No. Why? Doebuck seems to have befriended me."

"Sandro, he has only befriended you in order to hear your story. And unfortunately for you, in the telling you have sealed your fate."

"I do not understand."

"He has the bigger member. And he has breasts, so he is, as

the myths foretold: of great power, but like a woman born."

"So..."

The Publisher shook her head in frustration. "I do not understand how you can be so...oh well, it does not matter. The important thing is, Doebuck believes he is The Chosen One."

"Then he will kill me."

"Yes, and probably sooner rather than later. So...you must leave. You must follow me."

I hesitated. "But why should I trust you after what you did to me?"

"You should not, Sandro. But frankly, you have no choice." She unhooked my chain from the pole. "We must go...now!"

And so The Publisher led me back up through the ground toward the city. It was a long hard climb, and we were both tired when I again found myself in a damp, smelly sewer pipe. The Publisher climbed a metal ladder up to another opening, lifted the cover and looked out at the street. "Good," she whispered, "it is still dark in the city."

Then The Publisher climbed back down to me. "You must find Oswald, Oswald Goodie. He runs a club, The Queen's Revue, in the red zone. He will help you."

"Why?" I asked.

"Because he will know you are The Chosen One."

"You must come with me," I said.

"No," said The Publisher. "You tried to help me once and I only got you into trouble. This time I must act on my own. I will go back and kill Doebuck."

I was shocked. "Even if you do manage to kill him, you will also be killed."

The Publisher sighed. "The time has come for me to pay for my sins, Sandro. And they are many, and they are great.

"Maria may have told you I was not always so evil. Before I became part of this, I wanted to do good, to change things for the people. But I got caught up in the power, in my own brilliance, in...what difference does it make now? At least, if I go back and finish that man, or whatever he is, my death will redeem my soul. Now go, so I have time to return before he wakes up."

"I am sorry. I was wrong about you. Tell me, why have you done this for me?"

"Because I also believe you may well be The Chosen One, and I have secretly awaited you. If you are, the time of change is at hand. My only regret is I will not live to see The Great Overthrow. But think of me, and pray for me as the revolt progresses and my spirit will aid you."

As I climbed to my freedom, The Publisher grabbed my member and then kissed me for one last time.

Then the doomed woman lowered herself back down the ladder and she quickly returned to the underground where, I later heard she did complete her terrible task before she was hacked to pieces by the other members of the gang; and her flesh was cooked and eaten on the 1,763rd Day of the Drought at a feast celebrating the gang's belief that if they consumed her flesh in human sacrifice, Doebuck's body would return to life and lead them on a holy war to capture the shining city built above their underground cavern.

Rain

Chapter Ten: Reality

Reality is the core of an illusionary onion. As we peel back each layer we are only confronted with another slightly smaller illusion until we reach the center and find...nothing. So, after all our work, we are left, only, with many layers of illusion —as well as all the tears we cried as we peeled each illusion away.

But there are small white pearl onions and big fat red ones and soft old brown ones and pale yellow ones and bright green ones. After a while, the quest for reality becomes secondary, and we learn to enjoy each onion for itself. We give up the yearning after certainty and learn to appreciate the rich varieties of fantasy.

Oswald Goodie never concerned himself with reality. He was born and raised in illusion, a deformed cesarean cut away from a mother who adored him anyway. She raised little Oswald with great love and patient kindness, so his soul was never tormented by the taunts and insults whispered behind his mother's back when he was an infant, hurled in his face when he was a schoolboy, or used to vilify and destroy him as an adult. The sole effect of the world's revulsion was to drive Oswald into the Red Zone. There he opened a club where he only dealt in illusion.

Oswald was very tall and very fat, over 170 kilos. His blurry, yellow eyes were little dots surrounded by loose pockets of pale white skin. He had a large, flat porcine nose and no chin. His ears were disproportionately big, his breasts hung from his chest and rested against his enormous belly. His belly completely covered his member and stones. His entire body was covered with red and brown freckles.

Oswald's only redeeming physical qualities were, inexplicably, a pair of long and shapely legs that could only be called beautiful, and a full head of the most extraordinary wavy red hair. Actually, there was another: he had a rich, clear voice which could effectively sing the entire range from second tenor through baritone. And he loved to sing.

Oswald's club was called The Queen's Revue and it was located on a crooked little street off the main concourse in the Red Zone. It was not a large place, but it was crowded every night with patrons who came to see and hear the best female impersonators in Central City.

Oswald was the emcee, and he called himself Madame Piggly. He bound his upper body with specially built undergarments so that he was just able to fit into a large but tight gold lamé dress which was slit up the sides to show off his legs. He made up his face in a mask of its true appearance, and he had his hair cut at the most expensive salon in the zone. On stage, his grotesque proportions were transformed into a caricature of an amazonian, fading diva.

However, when I first saw Oswald, he was not on the stage. It was just after sunset, and the fierce, burning sun no longer made the pavement burn beneath my worn, bare feet as I crept through the narrow alleyways until I found the back door of The Queen's Revue. I rapped lightly. No one responded so I knocked again, and suddenly a mis-shapen giant appeared. He held onto a frilly little pink and yellow housecoat he had, more or less, wrapped around himself.

"I am looking for Oswald Goodie," I said.

"Do you sing or dance?"

"Neither," I said. "I was sent by...The Publisher." Mentioning

The Publisher made the giant very uncomfortable. "I am Oswald Goodie," he hissed, "Come inside...quickly."

I followed Oswald down a narrow hallway into a cramped dressing room where a number of men were in various stages of undress while they put on makeup and arranged their costumes.

"We can talk in here," said Goodie, "We are all members of the resisting classes."

As I told Oswald my story, he trembled when each new detail confirmed his suspicions about my true identity. But I was not really paying much attention to Oswald's excitement because I was fascinated as I looked around the room and watched the men go through their preparations.

They all had superb, beautiful bodies. Some had tightly muscled bottoms and wonderfully molded thighs and calves. Some of them had well-rounded pectorals that sat high on their chests, and light brown nipples covered with haloes of dark soft hair. Others shaved their chests and left them loose and soft so when they arranged them in their push-up undergarments they were sweetly rounded and full.

In a corner, by a full length mirror, a tall, thin man with small rounded buttocks, hard, flat belly and long expressive hands was shaving his intimate area with a straight razor. I was attracted to his highly defined hip joint, the kind fit young men have, the cleft on each side that led down, down to his groin. He spread his legs very wide while he sat on the edge of his chair; and, as he gracefully stroked each thigh with the sharp thin edge of the blade, he delicately lifted his member and his stones and moved them from one side to the other.

His organ was perfectly proportioned to the rest of his body—long and sleek and slender, and the foreskin had not been removed. His fingers softly stroked himself to keep fairly hard while he shaved close to the shaft.

He had short, straight black hair which he oiled and brushed back from his face, high Asian cheekbones, a square cleft chin and piercing blue eyes. His nose was a curved beak, curved and rounded to a point which made his face fierce, cruel and very exotic.

"He is from the high mountains to the north," said Goodie. His comment startled me because I did not realize I had been that obvious. "Do you find him handsome?" asked Goodie.

"Yes," I said.

"Then Ashmir is yours if you wish," said Goodie. "After all, you are the one."

"Why do you say that?" I asked him.

"Because it is true," said Goodie. "The rumors have reached us here, and your words confirm what we have been told. We know you are The Chosen One, and so we will help you and protect you."

Ashmir finished shaving and put on a tight purple garment. He forced his member back toward his body so he looked very flat in front. Then he applied black eyeliner, eye shadow and mascara. He reached for a tube of soft red lip color, painted each lip, pursed his lips and then traced the pattern with rust-colored liner.

His garter belt was purple silk and black lace. His stockings, black-on-black with swirling patterns of flowers and thick seams in the back. He rolled each stocking slowly up each leg. Then he attached them to the belt, patted his bottom, patted his belly and looked in the full-length mirror to gauge the effect. He reached for a matching purple and black padded strapless undergarment which he hooked in front and then adjusted so the cups sat properly on his chest. Again, he checked himself in the mirror.

Goodie again remarked on how much watching Ashmir

aroused me. "Why do you not talk to him?" said Goodie. I shook my head, no. Goodie shrugged as I involuntarily licked my dry lips and rubbed my sweating palms against each other.

Ashmir went to the dress rack and chose a simple, short black shift, cut very low in back. The material was cheap flimsy fabric, but on him it looked rather elegant and expensive. He completed his costume by choosing a pair of stiletto-heeled, knee-high, black leather boots. After one last glance in the mirror, he whirled around, walked over to me, kissed me hard on the lips and left. I gasped. My knees buckled momentarily. I did not know what to say or do.

Goodie laughed, and grabbed my hand. "Let us clean you up and prepare you for tomorrow's celebrations," he said. He took me to another room where there was a small tub of soapy water, and another of clear water. "It is not much," said Goodie, "but at least we have this little bit. You can wash off." He showed me a closet filled with men's and women's clothes. "Wear whatever suits your fancy," he said, and then he left me alone.

I pulled off the desert shorts the Shadowless Ones had given me and my torn, filthy shirt. I looked at my face in a small, cracked mirror near the soapy basin and I was shocked. My hair was a knotted, tangled mess; my skin was covered with dirt, grease and grit; my eyes were bloodshot; my lips were dry, chapped and burnt. It made me cry to see myself like that. I took a deep breath and then I felt a hand on my shoulder. It was Ashmir.

Ashmir did not speak to me, instead he guided me to the soapy basin. He pressed two fingers against my eyes, ladled a small cup of the soapy water and trickled it into my hair. His powerful sensitive fingers massaged and worked through my hair. Then he picked up a sponge and slowly, carefully rubbed all the filth from my forehead, from my face, my neck, back and chest.

While Ashmir worked on my body, I stood swaying from side to side under his strong but gentle touch. When he was satisfied I was clean, he went to the other basin, found another, softer sponge and again gently touched my forehead, my face, my neck, back and chest, and finally, my feet and toes.

I closed my eyes and let my body relax. Suddenly I felt soft wet skin on my member. I opened my eyes and looked down just as Ashmir stopped licking and instead took me into his mouth, drawing so deeply he was almost able, despite my size, to touch my stones with his lips. As he worshipped me, I crouched down and pulled his dress over his buttocks. When I stood and saw his perfect bottom again, I almost released but I forced myself to wait.

Meanwhile, Ashmir moved his mouth from my member to my stomach, then my nipples which he licked with the flat of his tongue and drew on until they were hard. Then he stood. He ran his hands through my hair, kissed me on the lips and extended his tongue all the way into my mouth. Then he stared into my eyes and smiled.

Ashmir pulled his black shift over his head, removed his undergarment but left his purple garters and black stockings on. Then he took my hand and walked me to the dressing table. He faced the mirror, spread his legs a bit and presented his beautiful bottom to me. I breathed deeply and moved against him, letting the tip of my flesh brush against him. He reached onto the dressing table, moistened his fingers with oil and spread the salve against his entrance. I pushed forward and rubbed my member against him. Ashmir slowly moved back toward me, pressing the head of my flesh into his body.

Gradually, I moved deeper and deeper inside of him, grabbed his waist and watched in the mirror as he moved and writhed against me. I reached around, pulled down his garment and grabbed one of his nipples between my thumb and index finger. As I squeezed harder and harder, Ashmir moaned and arched his back and whispered for me to lick his neck.

As my tongue moved across the straining muscles of his shoulders, then up beneath his hairline, Ashmir released and I watched his pure white seed splash against the image of us reflected in the mirror. At that point, I could wait no more. I pulled myself out of Ashmir, and I released all over his naked back. He turned, smiled, reached up and gently drew away the last few drops that remained on the head of my member.

Ashmir then stood and whispered in my ear: "You must lead us forward to the Overthrow."

I sighed. Ashmir's personal appeal after such passion truly moved me.

"If it means so much to you...to you and all the others," I said, "then I will do whatever you want me to do...or at least I will do what I can. But..."

Ashmir touched my shoulder. He said, "You are The Chosen One are you not?"

I do not know why, but for the very first time, I answered yes to that question.

"I am so happy," Ashmir said. "Sandro, I have waited for this day for such a long time. I would not...would not, after so many years, want to make a mistake."

Something in Ashmir's voice when he said 'mistake' frightened me. I looked into Ashmir's fierce, angry eyes. "What do you mean, a mistake?"

Ashmir only smiled and kissed me on my cheek. "What is that talisman you wear around your neck?"

For some reason I did not tell him the truth. "My parents gave it to me when I left home," I told him. He believed me of course, bowed and then left.

I went to the closet and found a clean white cotton shirt

and a pair of baggy white cotton pants. There were no socks, but a pair of soft brown sandals fit me perfectly.

When Oswald Goodie rejoined me, he was in his gold lamé dress, ready to appear on stage. He fussed over me, remarking on the improvement in my looks and demeanor. "Ah, yes, you look much better...You will create a much better impression...Sandro, I think they all might believe now..." Goodie muttered as he clattered around me in his oversized heels. When he seemed satisfied, he stopped his fussing and stood facing me.

"Ashmir asked me if he could be your personal bodyguard during the parade," said Oswald.

"What parade?" I asked.

"Once a year, tomorrow morning in fact, at sunrise, all the resisting classes meet at the Cathedral of The Living Truth to celebrate the Feast of Joy. The authorities permit it. That is why The Publisher sent you to me."

"But what about the parade?"

"After the service at the cathedral, we march in procession to the Central Square. Once there, we present our grievances to the authorities. They also permit that. It serves a useful function for them."

"And then?"

"Well, of course, every other year, after we present our grievances, the authorities acknowledge them, enter them into the record, and then we go home."

I knew what was coming, but I had to ask. "But not tomorrow?"

"No, not tomorrow," Goodie agreed. He stared at me with a certain longing. "Tomorrow the resisting classes will actually resist," he said. "Tomorrow, on the 1,766th Day of the Drought, we will begin the Overthrow. It will be a glorious day, a truly glorious day. But it will also be a very dangerous day. That is why you may need a bodyguard, and why you... why you..." Suddenly, the gentle giant broke down. He tottered on his high heels, then kicked them away and dropped to his knees. He fell before me, and kissed my feet.

"You will lead us in the Overthrow," Oswald Goodie's voice broke as he spoke those words. Then he sighed, took a deep breath and said, "Rain will fill the skies. We will return water to the people and we will again have life."

I helped Oswald to his feet and embraced him. For all his grotesque appearance, there was something noble about this man who had created beauty from ugliness, who had built a sanctuary for outcasts, who believed so deeply in redemption. "I will do what I can," I told him. "I promise you that much."

"That is all anyone can ask," said Oswald. He wiped tears from his yellow eyes and straightened his dress. "Now I must prepare. The show must go on, as they say. Even on the eve of revolution, we must give them beauty and illusion."

"May I watch?" I asked.

Oswald beamed. "Of course! You are our honored guest."

He led me through a narrow passage to the wings of the small stage. The theater itself was packed with people of all descriptions, workers still in their dusty clothes, merchants in their finery, soldiers out of uniform, even a few well-dressed individuals who might have been from the inner circles slumming in the Red Zone. The air was thick with smoke and anticipation.

The lights dimmed, and Oswald Goodie, now Madame Piggly, swept onto the stage in a glory of gold lamé and red hair. His voice, that magnificent instrument, filled the small theater as he sang an old ballad about lost love and distant rains. The audience fell silent, mesmerized. In that moment, his physical grotesqueness disappeared, and all that remained was the pure beauty of sound and yearning.

As I watched Ashmir dance across the stage in a later number, his body moving with liquid grace despite the stiletto heels, I understood what Oswald had been trying to tell me about illusion and reality. Perhaps The Chosen One was also an illusion, a story we told ourselves to give meaning to suffering, a mask we put on to face the unbearable. But if the illusion gave people hope, if it moved them to action, was it not as real as anything else?

Tomorrow would be the 1,766th Day of the Drought. Tomorrow the Overthrow would begin. And tomorrow I would discover whether I was truly The Chosen One, or simply another desperate soul playing a part in a grand and possibly tragic illusion.

Then the stage manager moved down the hall knocking on doors and calling out, "Show time...show time."

Goodie stumbled to his feet as best he could and joined the others as they headed for the stage and the opening number of that night's second performance.

Rain

Chapter Eleven: Religion

Religion is a sexual experience. All religious texts speak of gods entering us, of the marriage of man or woman with God, and of the ultimate transcendent union of humans and gods. All religions bless and sanctify those individuals who achieve a mystical communion with God. All religious ceremony brings people to a place where they join together, and where they willingly, sometimes enthusiastically, give up their individuality in the passion of group yearning and celebration.

The most powerful religions are those that most effectively arouse their supplicants to the greatest passion. The most powerful ministers are those who preach the word directly to the groins and loins of their congregations. The happiest congregations are those that sweep the worshipers away from the cares and trials of their daily lives into a sanctuary where there is no pain, no loneliness, no suffering.

The protesting classes who worshipped at the Cathedral of The Living Truth had nothing to place in the offering basket except their desperate hope. The cathedral was the place where the sick and the poor and the lost, the weird and the bizarre and the failed, the weak and the disenfranchised and the ineffectual, the dreamers and the fanatics and the believers, the losers and the downtrodden and the deprived came to celebrate the Feast of Joy. And each year, for a few hours, they found meaning, their lives had purpose, their prayers were answered.

The pastor of the cathedral was the Reverend Brother

Armando Armandini. When he was not in clerical garb and before the altar, he was not a particularly remarkable man. One could pass him on the street and feel nothing, except perhaps a pleasant tingling sensation as one brushed past the power of his aura.

Ah, but when he spoke, when he stood in front of the massive marble columns, beneath the golden canopy, under the windows of light, then...then Armando Armandini was God to his congregation.

As Goodie and Ashmir had requested, I stood among those masses of hot, sweaty bodies and expectant faces that had gathered on that very special Feast of Joy that occurred on the 1,766th Day of the Drought. I, too, looked toward the altar when Reverend Brother Armandini turned, raised his hands, blessed the congregation and intoned, from deep within his chest, the words: "Today, my children, the moment for which we have waited, The Overthrow we have sought...has... come." He dramatically dropped his hands and let his head fall against his chest as if the enormity of what he was going to say utterly overwhelmed him, "Today is our day. Today is The Great Overthrow."

The congregation became a hornets' nest. The buzzing and murmuring grew louder and louder while Armandini stood silently staring out across the heads of his congregation. Then he raised his arms again and the noise stopped. He spoke: "Feel the joy, my children! Feel the joy! Truly I say unto you: The Great Overthrow is near!" Then he collapsed in a heap at the foot of the altar and said no more.

The cathedral erupted in pandemonium. The buzzing noise turned into an audible chant, "Brothers and sisters, know no fear. The Great Overthrow is near." One group started clapping in rhythm to the chant. Soon, the whole congregation was chanting and clapping and dancing in place. The combined effect felt like an earthquake, and I feared the building might collapse on top of us.

Then the floor-to-ceiling doors at the rear of the church opened, and the congregation spilled out into the street. Two enormous men carried Armandini out of the church through the frantic tens of thousands gathering in front of the cathedral. Gradually, everyone formed a line eight or ten abreast behind the Reverend Brother, and then they proceeded up the main boulevard toward the Central Square about five kilometers away.

Even in the searing mid-day heat, the people in the procession continued to chant and clap and dance in unison. As they moved closer to the square, their excitement increased and any semblance of discipline broke down completely. The line fell apart, people spoke in tongues, some tore off their clothing, others fainted, still others screamed and shook in frightening fits.

By the time the procession arrived at the square, it was obvious the authorities had received advance warning and were already preparing for an unusual Feast of Joy. Loudspeakers ringed the square as they always did. The red and yellow banners of the protesting classes hung from the buildings, and red and yellow bunting decorated the stage as it always did. The doors of the Great Hall were left open, as they always were, for the presentation of grievances. But the entire square was surrounded by a triple-deep line of baton-wielding, helmeted Authoritarian Guards. They had never, ever been there before.

Despite the presence of the guards, the frenzied crowd continued moving into the square, and even those who may have preferred to try to escape because they realized the situation was extremely dangerous were resigned to the fact that there was really no hope for escape. More and more people jammed into the square. The increasing tension and excitement raised the crowd to absolutely insane heights.

I asked Goodie if the celebrations were always like the one we were seeing. "No, no," said Goodie, "this is more people than I have ever seen for a Feast of Joy. The rumors have spread throughout Central City."

"What rumors?" I asked.

"The rumors that The Chosen One will lead The Great Overthrow," said Ashmir. When he said it, he looked at me with those fierce blue eyes, and I felt a chill despite the heat.

Flasks of a dark blue liquid were passed from hand to hand. Everyone drank, although its acrid taste lingered on the tongue and no one took more than one swallow. I hesitated when the flask reached me, but Goodie urged me on. "You must drink," he whispered. "It is part of the ritual." The liquid burned going down and left a strange metallic taste in my mouth. Within moments, I felt its effects, my skin became more sensitive, colors grew more vivid, and a warm euphoria spread through my body.

Then the chanting began again, and the crowd's mood escalated toward delirium.

Everyone tore at each other's clothing, and within minutes everyone was virtually naked. Then, as if on some commonly recognized signal, everyone began to grab and kiss and touch everyone else. Men were stroking each other's members, women were placing their fingers inside each other, men and women were bending over and pulling hard flesh into their openings, men were drawing on and squeezing whatever breasts they could touch, women and men were taking throbbing, wet members in their mouths, women were pinching their hard nipples and crying out, men were furiously working their flesh as they jumped up and down and watched their seed fly through the air. And still the chanting grew even louder: "Brothers and sisters, know no fear...today the Great Overthrow is here."

Suddenly I found myself surrounded by a family of acrobats, a grandfather, three sons, their wives and a granddaughter in her late teens. All the men had the high cheekbones, black hair and short, stocky bodies of the southern tribes who lived beyond the edge of the Great Desert. The women, except for the granddaughter, were tall, round-faced, dimpled blondes from the northern rain forests.

The granddaughter was the perfect mix of the two strains, high cheekbones and dark hair but round blue eyes, tall but well-muscled, broad shouldered, but with a tiny waist. She stood naked on her grandfather's shoulders. He randomly tossed her into the air by squatting and then leaping as high as he could. She simultaneously leapt from his shoulders. The granddaughter achieved such height she performed a full flip with a twist before she landed back on her grandfather's shoulders. Her tight little breasts did not bounce at all and her buttocks did not ripple. The tendons in her long legs stretched and strained. Her painted toes gripped her grandfather's collarbone. But she did not falter or sway.

Then the two oldest brothers and their wives began to caress each other until the two men's thick members were clearly erect. The two blondes turned and faced each other, threw their arms around each other's necks and licked each other's tongues. As they kissed, they arched their backs and presented themselves so their husbands could enter them from behind.

Then the other brother and his wife climbed onto the shoulders of the two brothers who were joining with their wives. That couple faced each other, grabbed each other's arms and jutted their bodies into each other so the man's member just entered a few centimeters into his wife's opening. Within seconds, all three couplings managed to achieve a rhythm that allowed them all to move in and out of each other.

At that point the grandfather shouted for his granddaughter to again stand on his shoulders. Then he lowered himself into a squat so low his stones actually touched the ground, took a deep breath and then exhaled as he shot into the air. At the peak of his acceleration, the granddaughter also launched herself with an extraordinary effort. As she sailed into the air she did a double somersault and landed at the top of the pyramid with one foot on her blond mother's shoulder and the other balanced on the shoulder of her dark-haired father. Then she began to undulate her hips suggestively, pleasure herself and run her hands up and down her body. The grandfather danced in front, and his moans and swinging member became the rhythm by which they all kept time. The entire pyramid swayed in perfect unison, back and forth, back and forth, the members sliding in and out, the blondes' breasts bouncing, the young body on top teasing and taunting the crowd, back and forth, back and forth...

Then, when they all eight climaxed together in one release, the crowd went wild. I felt the blue liquid coursing through my veins, amplifying every sensation, every sight, every sound. The entire square seemed to pulse with life and desire.

Meanwhile, the Authoritarian Guards seemed unsure of what to do. Some of them were overcome with excitement by what they were watching. They tore off their uniforms and entered into the ritual. Others were shocked and upset by what they saw and, giving in to the blood lust of their own peculiar excitement, waded into the crowd with their batons to break bones, crack heads and splatter blood, although these attacks did not have the effect on the crowd which the guards may have intended.

However, most of the guards simply stood, and watched... and waited. I felt Oswald's hand on my shoulder. "It is time," said Oswald, "You must join the Reverend Brother Armandini on the stage."

Oswald and Ashmir struggled forward toward the stage, with me in tow, through the teeming masses of the writhing, sweating, twisting congregation. As I climbed the stairs onto the stage and approached the Reverend Armando Armandini, Armandini opened out his arms, turned his palms up and smiled so deeply his aura leapt into the space between him and me and then drew me toward him. When we embraced, Armandini whispered in my ear, "Thank you for this moment, Sandro. I did not think I would live to see it."

Then Armandini turned me toward the crowd and raised his right arm into the air. The crowd roared and screamed and whistled. Armandini smiled, hugged me again and kissed me on both cheeks. That time he whispered a warning in my ear, "Sandro, when I am gone, beware the traitor's kiss."

His words confused me, but before I could ask what he meant, Armandini let go of my arm, fell to his knees and prostrated himself in front of me. The crowd was delirious with happiness, and once again the entire crowd loudly took up the chant: "Brothers and sisters know no fear. Today the Great Overthrow is near." Armandini raised his head off the ground, rose to his knees and began to stand, but he never made it.

The last I saw of Armandini was the beatific vision on the Reverend Brother's face before it exploded in a crimson mass of shattered bone, torn flesh and scrambled brains. One of Armandini's eyeballs rolled across the stage and fell into the crowd below.

That is when the Authoritarian Guards moved on cue. They hacked and smashed their way across the square, but the crowd was so drugged by the blue narcotic and their passion they were unaware they were under attack. Bodies flew in every direction. I saw the acrobat family go down from the blows of a particularly vicious guard. He focused on inflicting maximum pain on the granddaughter, and it was terrible to see that beautiful young child beaten so savagely.

For a few moments, those of us on the stage were suspended in time and space, floating above the ugliness and cruelty below. I desperately tried to analyze an escape route through the crowd, but I quickly realized even if I could get through the mangled bodies, every avenue was blocked, every alley was sealed off.

Then a small group of guards climbed onto the stage, and quickly surrounded our small group. Oswald Goodie, that unfortunate, gentle giant, let out a cry and charged at the approaching guards. He did not get three meters before they cut him down. I watched him fall, his gold lamé dress billowing around him like a deflating balloon, his beautiful legs crumpling beneath his enormous weight. Even in death, he was grotesque and magnificent at once.

At that point, all the rest of us realized the futility of any further resistance. We raised our hands in surrender, and the leader of the guards said, "We have come for The Chosen One."

When the guard said that, Ashmir (I could not believe it but it was true) Ashmir walked up to me and kissed me hard on the lips. "This is he who claims to be the one you wish to find," Ashmir said to the guards. "Seize him and remove the cord and talisman from around his neck."

As they grabbed me and ripped away my magic, I tried to look for a reason in Ashmir's eyes, to try to understand. "Why?" I cried.

Ashmir simply laughed. Then, as he walked away, he turned around and said, "Oh, false prophet, know great fear...for the Day of your Overthrow is already here."

I screamed after him, "You used me! You knew all along!" But Ashmir had already disappeared into the chaos of bodies and blood.

The guards bound my hands behind my back and began to drag me off the stage. As I stumbled down the steps, I looked back one last time at the square. What had been a celebration of hope and ecstasy had become a scene of absolute carnage. The chanting had turned to screaming. The dancing had become the writhing of the wounded and dying. Blood pooled on the cobblestones, mixing with other fluids from the interrupted ritual.

And above it all, the red and yellow banners of the protesting classes still fluttered in the hot wind, a mockery of everything the day had promised.

I had failed them. I had led them to slaughter. Whether I was truly The Chosen One or simply a fraud who had allowed himself to be used, the result was the same. Thousands were dead or dying, and I was being dragged away to face whatever fate The Inquisitor had prepared for me.

As we moved through the crowd, people reached out to touch me, some in anger, blaming me for the disaster; others in desperate hope, still believing I could somehow save them. But I could do nothing. Without my talisman, I was just a man. Just Sandro. No magic, no prophecy, no power to change anything.

The guards loaded me into a black wagon, and as the door slammed shut, cutting off the sounds of the dying, I finally understood what the Voice of the Shadowless Ones had been trying to tell me. The question was never whether I was truly The Chosen One. The question was whether I could become what the people needed me to be.

And on the 1,766th Day of the Drought, I had my answer: I had not.

Chapter Twelve: Torture

Threatening someone with death is not a particularly effective form of torture. After all, a painful death is not nearly as frightening as a painful life. Certain death means the pain will end; a long life means the pain will go on interminably.

Imagine a life in which each moment of every day is filled with the most excruciating pain, constant humiliation and debilitating fear. That is why victims of physical torture often live in misery long enough to realize they will survive, then they commit suicide.

So, to be effective, torture must inflict the maximum pain necessary to create fear without mortally wounding the victim. Of course there are myths and legends about those heroic individuals who do not talk. Of course those myths and legends are nonsense. Everyone talks.

Everyone talks because the mind and the will are not so strong. If one's mind and one's will could exist independent of one's body, then secrecy might have a fighting chance. But our frail flesh, if properly attacked, will always sell out our mind and our will in order to save itself.

That is why the best torturers are geniuses at inflicting precise levels of physical pain, and why Tokorotan was considered a virtuoso performer. It was said he only needed twenty five minutes with a person to know their vulnerable points, then two hours maximum to extract the information. In my case, he needed less than fourteen minutes to get it all.

My problem was that without my magic I did not see any

point in telling him a lie, but he would not believe what I told him was really the truth. So instead of being what I actually was, one of Tokorotan's easiest victims, he thought I was one of his most difficult. And I was in the unenviable position of trying to invent ever more elaborate lies so Tokorotan would be convinced I was telling him the truth and either stop hurting me...or kill me. At a certain point, I really did not care which.

Tokorotan was a little man, short and very thin. He had beautiful wide brown eyes, a rounded nose and pointed chin. His lips were thin, and when he spoke they stretched back from his mouth to reveal a full set of straight, white teeth. He shaved his head, his entire head: He had no beard, mustache, hair or even eyebrows.

He worked in a bare concrete basement room from which no sound could escape, although I was well aware the room served another purpose because I experienced how frightening it was to hear my own screams reverberate off the cold, hard walls.

Tokorotan began his questioning innocently enough, by entering the room calmly, shutting the door behind him and sitting on the edge of a simple wooden table.

"Why were you arrested?" Tokorotan asked.

I responded that I assumed it was because I was being called The Chosen One and I was supposed to lead something called the Great Overthrow.

Tokorotan stood and kicked my chair out from under me in one swift powerful blow. My bottom landed hard on the stone floor. Tokorotan smiled and his brown eyes sparkled.

He again asked me why I was arrested, and again I told him I assumed it was because I was said to be The Chosen One, and I had been on the stage at the Feast of Joy.

"Do you in fact believe you are The Chosen One?" Tokorotan asked.

"No, I do not believe it," I said, "although maybe you do. It seems everyone else does."

Tokorotan appeared pleased. He embraced me, held my head between the palms of his hands and stared into my eyes. He kissed me on both cheeks, mussed up my hair and then struck me in the mouth so hard he knocked out two of my front teeth. I spit out blood and tooth enamel.

"What I believe, or what I do not believe is not the issue here, my dear Sandro," said Tokorotan. He then asked me for a third time why I believed I had been arrested, and so I told him the following story.

"I was working for The Director of Finance. I was sent to pick up a packet from The Publisher just before she defected to the underground. I know she defected because I actually helped her defect. Then I was arrested on the street for breaking curfew and tortured by The Inquisitor who tattooed my member and sent me to the Superdump. I escaped the Superdump and ended up on the Great Desert where a voice told me I was The Chosen One and sent me back to Central City. When I arrived in the city, I went to The Queen's Revue where I met Oswald Goodie and a man called Ashmir. They told me I really was The Chosen One, and I was to lead the Great Overthrow. Goodie was killed. Ashmir betrayed me. Now I am here before you."

Tokorotan told me to take off my clothes which I did. Then he had me sit naked on the stone floor. He stood over me, unbuckled his pants, pulled out his member and urinated all over me. His waste mingled with my blood in pools on the floor.

"I urinate on your story," said Tokorotan. "First of all, The Publisher did not defect. No one from the Inner Circle ever defects. She was brutally murdered by members of a secret underground cell. We are, at this very moment, erecting a statue in her memory in the Central Square."

"If you say so," I mumbled.

Tokorotan pulled me up off the ground by my hair and threw me back into my chair. Then he went to a simple metal cabinet, returned with various straps and proceeded to strap me into the chair. Then he brought a shaving mug and a dirty, rusted straight razor from the cabinet. As I trembled in fear, Tokorotan shaved my head, making sure that he cut me quite often and that I saw and felt the blood running down my face.

Tokorotan took off his shirt, stood behind me, leaned down and rubbed his chest against my back. At first, I found Tokorotan's touch a curiously relaxing sensation. Then he suddenly clapped both hands hard against my ears. The incredible pain sent shock waves through my body.

Tokorotan continued: "Second of all, there is no one called The Inquisitor. I am the only agent authorized to interrogate prisoners. And there is no detention camp called the Superdump, and even if there was such a place, if it was run by the Central Authorities it would have been impossible for you to escape from there."

Tokorotan returned to sitting on the edge of his table. He stared at me for a few minutes. Then he took off the rest of his clothes, and I noticed he had an erection. He was also breathing heavily, but he only stared and smiled and occasionally rubbed my head.

After a few more minutes spent studying me, Tokorotan again spoke: "Three thousand people died yesterday at the Feast of Joy. This is the worst case of public disorder we have experienced in...in a long time."

Tokorotan went back to his little cabinet and returned with an electronic device with two copper wires which he attached to my stones. Then he turned the crank, slowly at first.

It was strange, but the initial low voltage was stimulating, and I discovered, to my horror and surprise, that, even though my member had returned to its normal size, I was getting an erection. When Tokorotan saw my arousal he became enraged and immediately cranked the machine faster. I still did not feel real pain, and my member was completely erect.

Tokorotan screamed: "There is no such person as The Chosen One! You are just a man, and a stupid, weak foolish man at that!"

He then raised the voltage to its highest level, and the pain was so great, I actually broke two of my straps as I lifted my chair completely off the ground. When Tokorotan stopped turning the crank, I could smell burning flesh. When I looked down, I saw that my stones were badly burned.

Tokorotan restrapped me into my chair. "Who are you! What is your real mission!"

I shouted at the top of my lungs: "My mission is to avenge the death of my lover and assassinate the Supreme Leader."

Tokorotan was delighted. "Very good, very, very goooooood. Yes, to assassinate the Supreme Leader. Now we have something."

I was close to losing consciousness, but at least I had hit upon something he seemed to want. But Tokorotan was still dissatisfied. "And so...so how were you going to accomplish this assassination?"

"Uh...with a hand weapon," I said. "Yes, with a pistol."

Tokorotan picked up the rusty old razor again, walked over to me, pinched my right nipple and with a flick of his wrist, sliced it off. Blood spurted from my chest.

I know now I must have fainted because the next time I looked at my breast there was a surgical clamp where my nipple used to be and the bleeding had stopped.

Tokorotan growled, "Everyone knows the Supreme Leader

cannot be killed by a mere weapon. Tell me the truth." I frantically tried to remember the myths and legends I had heard from Mariann and Alexander. How was it said the Supreme Leader was supposed to die?

Meanwhile, Tokorotan was yelling in my ear, "How were you to accomplish this assassination?"

I could not think of anything. My body screamed with pain. My mind was a blur. My spirit was broken. Finally a phrase came to me, "With the water of life and a silver sword!"

Tokorotan was triumphant. "Yes, yes...And where were you going to get the water of life?"

I broke down and whimpered, "I do not know. I do not remember anything else."

"Who has the silver sword? Who? You will tell me, dear Sandro. You will tell me!"

Tokorotan picked up a braided leather whip with tiny pieces of metal woven into the thongs. "Where is the water of life?" he screamed as I felt the whip's lash on my shoulders, once twice, three times.

"Who has the silver sword?"

Again his terrible whip lashed against my back. Then again... and again. I screamed, but my panic only pushed Tokorotan to greater fury as he whipped my entire body.

From that point on everything I saw happened in slow motion through a purple haze. My blood and little pieces of my skin were flying everywhere. Tokorotan was dancing and skipping from side to side, his member in one hand, the whip in his other. His eyes were glazed, opaque. His lips quivered. His breathing came in short little gasps.

Then Tokorotan completely lost control. He put down the whip and picked up the razor. He stabbed me on my feet. He sliced through my hand. He cut my stones. With each bloodletting his desire rose even higher, and at the moment he began his release, he grabbed the whip again and beat as hard as he could. I vaguely remember Tokorotan's seed landing on my head and back. And I was, more than anything...relieved it was over. As I slumped down in my chair, I knew I was dying, and it felt good to die while life splashed over me. Then everything was darkness.

But I did not die. I awakened on a cot covered with dirty, yellow sheets in a filthy room. The paint was peeling off the walls and ceiling. The windows were so greasy and brown they barely allowed light into the room. The place reeked of ammonia, sulfur and kerosene.

A gnarled little man with a stoop shuffled over to the bed and tried to focus his squinting, bloodshot eyes on me. Even through my fog and pain, I was pretty sure I recognized the man. He wore a long white medical smock and he rubbed his hands together as he spoke, "Ah, yes, so, Sandro, I think you will be fine, no?"

"Doctor Pritowski?"

I tried to say more, but my mouth would not open and my throat burned. I tried moving my right arm, found it worked and lifted the filthy sheet. A slow, cautious inventory revealed the horrible truth: I was a mass of scars and bruises and infected, torn flesh. I was missing two toes on my right foot and one on my left, one of my stones, a nipple and three fingers on my left hand. I cried.

The doctor was distressed to see my tears. He rubbed his hands together faster and faster. "At least you are alive," he said, "and soon you will be free."

I again tried to speak, but I could only manage a few moans. The doctor left me and returned with a small cup filled with red juice. I drank a little, and then I tried to focus on the old doctor.

"Yes, Sandro."

"How...how did you get here?"

"After The Publisher killed Doebuck and we had then killed The Publisher and eaten her flesh, things got pretty wild down there. When Doebuck did not come back to life, I was fairly certain we would not have much of an army to try to conquer Central City. I figured, well, so much for my earthly paradise, and I returned to the surface."

"Then you are alive, are you not. I mean, I am alive am I not? Or is this...is this..."

"You are alive, Sandro. And I am alive because they believe I have information that is...valuable to them."

I slumped back against my mattress. "I would rather be dead."

The old doctor sat on the edge of my bed and made an awkward attempt to hold my damaged hands. "But Sandro, you are alive, and you are the last hope for the underground. The word has spread everywhere that you are The Chosen One. You must live, if not for yourself then for the rest of us, and I will do what I can to save you."

"I am not The Chosen One, Doctor. You know that."

"I know nothing anymore." He let go of my hands. "I have done the best for you I can, Sandro. I have no good instruments here, and no place to do things right. I am old, Sandro, and I cannot see well. I am sorry. We must get you out of here. You must return to the arroyo to be healed."

I shook my head violently back and forth. "I do not want to live like this. Please, please, Pritowski, just let me die."

"I cannot do that, Sandro." The doctor held up a syringe and filled it with amber liquid. "I must put you to sleep now, but when you wake up, we will be out of here."

I tried to avoid the injection but I did not even have the strength to defy a broken old man. As the fluid entered my veins I immediately became drowsy. I looked up into the face of the doctor who looked down at me as if through a haze and said, "Whoever you are, whether you are The Chosen One or not, I hope when the time comes you will forgive all of us for what we have done to you."

I was soon fast asleep. I dreamed I was floating on a white cloud outside on the streets of the city. It was nighttime and there was a full moon. I was naked. Then the cloud disappeared, and I was alone on the hard ground, but I did not know where.

I was curled up on the pavement in a back lane or alley. There was garbage everywhere, and the pavement was still warm from the day's heat. The moonlight was bright enough for me to see the stumps where my fingers had been. I smelled a terrible odor which at first I thought was coming from the garbage. Then I realized I was smelling myself.

I tried to move but I could not. I tried to scream, but I could not. I tried to cry, but I could not. I desperately tried to make the pain go away, but of course I could not.

It was then that I realized I was not dreaming. On the 1,777th Day of the Drought, I really had been carried outside wrapped in a sheet and then dumped in an alley and left to survive as best I could.

I lay there for what might have been hours or might have been days. Time had lost all meaning. The only constants were pain and the slow realization that I was broken beyond repair. The Chosen One, if he had ever existed, was dead. What remained was simply Sandro, mutilated, abandoned, stripped of everything that had once made him whole.

And yet, even in that darkest moment, some small part of me refused to surrender. Perhaps it was the talisman's magic still lingering in my blood, even though the talisman itself was gone. Perhaps it was the memory of Mariann and Alexander's sacrifice, or Oswald's brave charge, or even The Publisher's final redemption. Perhaps it was simply the stubborn animal will to survive that lives in all flesh.

Whatever it was, I clung to it as the sun rose on the 1,778th Day of the Drought, and I was still alive.

Rain

Chapter Thirteen: Despair

Despair is the only state from which salvation is impossible. The closest feeling to despair is the feeling we feel when we have been rejected by a lover. Except, when we suffer from despair, we have not just lost love, we have lost life itself. To feel despair is to feel completely alone, totally abandoned and without a shred of hope. In fact, despair's only logical conclusion is self-destruction.

As I lay there in the alley, amongst the filth of which the filthiest was me, I was thinking about the different ways I could try to kill myself. Then Pritowski returned. The doctor was pushing an old peddler's cart filled with rags. He managed, despite my screams, to drag me onto the cart and cover me with the rags. Then we began the long hot journey to La Bruja's cabin. When we finally arrived at her dusty arroyo, I was delirious and dehydrated. My infections were worse. I was running a high, burning fever, and I was very near death.

Pritowski helped La Bruja carry me inside her hut where they placed me on the ground next to the fire. La Bruja brought salves and ointments from her shelves and covered my entire body with one yellow greasy liquid and then each of my scars with another brown one. Then she threw a mixture from a black clay jar onto the fire and the cabin filled with thick medicinal smoke. She held my head in her arms, and forced a narcotic tea down my throat. Then she told Pritowski to leave the cabin, and gave him instructions to find Maria and bring her to the cabin in three days.

The doctor raised his bushy white eyebrows. "I do not think he will live for three days, La Bruja. We must find out what he knows now, while we have the chance."

La Bruja was angry. "You know nothing about these things, you old goat. I said three days. He will be...ready."

When Pritowski left, La Bruja began to chant: "Wyudrluck froidb noutra quoondoos..."

And those were the last words I remember hearing for a long time. I had managed to escape from the pain and agony of my life by drifting off into my own field of dreams where I found happiness, comfort and protection from evil through a magic far greater than any La Bruja could provide.

I slipped slowly backward through time into dreams of my life on the green, growing plains far beyond the great desert, past even the high mountains.

I wrapped myself in memories of the damp, humid air and the smell of wet grass at night after the dew settled on the gentle valleys of my home country. I remembered lying awake at night and listening to the frenetic buzzing of the cicadas, the soft laughter from a dwelling down the street, animal noises...

My mother and father slept on a summer bed outside on warm nights, and I would often climb out of my window down a thick vine and hide in the bushes where I could watch them make love when they thought I was asleep.

My mother was a slim, dark-haired beauty with bright green eyes and an easy smile. My father was tall and handsome with silver hair on his temples, dark brown eyes and a thin salt and pepper mustache above his lip.

My mother would sit on the edge of their bed in her thin white nightgown which teased my father with glimpses of her large, soft, pink areolas and her triangle of soft curly hair.

My father was always naked. He had a very large member, and when my mother excited him, his flesh immediately grew hard and created a large tent under the thin single sheet that covered their bed.

My father would usually approach my mother from the front, and carefully, intently pull her nightgown down across her shoulders to expose her smooth, white breasts. Then he would bury his head between those gorgeous mounds and moan softly in the warm summer night.

My mother would sigh, hold my father's head in both her arms and run her fingers through his silver hair. Then she would slowly, gently push my father's head down onto her stomach where she cradled it against the soft hairs surrounding her navel. She would smile and watch his tongue lick her lower belly. Then she would guide him again, down toward her sex, and I would watch my mother shake and shiver as my father's tongue entered her.

They would remain like that, my father's head moving between my mother's legs, she twisting and squirming and pulling my father's head against her, until she climaxed in a wonderful release, and I would touch myself as I watched her moving all over the summer bed.

Then, while my mother was catching her breath, my father would climb onto the bed. Then my mother would take my father's throbbing member in her mouth, and draw on it, and squeeze it, and caress it, and lick it while she looked up into his eyes and he down at hers, until his movements indicated he was going to release, and then she liked to hold his member out in front of her and let his wet white fluid shower her face and her breasts and her undulating belly...

Time passed. The thick smoke entered my lungs and the salves penetrated my skin. The brown ointment sealed my wounds, but I did not know those things were happening to me. Time passed in dreams and mind wanderings away, away from the cabin, La Bruja and my fever.

I wandered even further back, back to when I discovered the girl next door undressing by candlelight with her curtains open and her tender body naked and young and soft and fresh...

I used to sit in my darkened room and marvel at her flesh, so different from my own, and I was surprised how much she excited me. I would sit for hours stroking my recently developed member and wonder at my incredibly good fortune to have this beautiful girl undress for me.

Each night she would enter her room fully clothed and move in front of her dressing area where there was a large round mirror. Then she would sit in front of the mirror and take the pins out of her thick long brown hair which fell across her shoulders down her back to her waist. Then, with her back still toward me, she would take off her shirt and toss it on the floor, and I was left to imagine myself licking her naked back.

Then she would reach down and take off her sandals. After that she usually would stand up and slip out of her skirt. She would untie her skirt at her waist, and lean forward which pushed her bottom out toward me as I watched her. Then she would bend one leg while she slipped the other over the waistband of her skirt, stand on one leg like a graceful bird, then shift to the other leg and lift her skirt free.

Most of the time she stayed in her undergarments while she paraded around her room one more time. Then she would pick up her clothes and fold them. She would rearrange things on her dresser. She would brush out her hair. She would pull back the covers of her bed.

And then...then she would stand in the middle of the window with her body in profile, and ever so slowly, slowly hook her thumbs under the fabric of her garment and slide it down, down her long, young legs. And then, as she did so, she would lean forward and her pert little breasts would peek out from beneath her hair, and then, when her garment was off and she stood up again, and her hair again covered those long-nippled treats, I could just see the soft, downy brown hairs of her young sex. The first time I caught her performance was also the very first time I ever released, and I released afterwards each time I saw her, and perhaps I even released again as I remembered...

And only La Bruja knew whether I actually released again or not. Only she knew whether I did really feel those things I saw inside my head while I was dreaming and time was passing and I was able to forget I was wounded and mutilated and scared, and I only had a lonely, mysterious sorceress to comfort me.

I remembered the autumn when the leaves turned yellow, red and gold, when the nights were cold and sharp but the days were sunny warm and clear, when clean winds blew in from the northwest and the fields were bare but our tables were filled with smoked meat and new potatoes and fresh vegetables and hot baked breads and berry pies and fruit jams and dark sweet beers and plum wine, and the people were happy, and life was fine for those who lived on the central plains.

And I remembered the best fall of them all when I fell in love with a girl from a nearby town who came to the fall festival in a light blue gown and pony cart decorated in banners of gold, green and orange. She wore blue ribbons in her hair and her eyes were as blue as the crystal clear fall sky was blue, and her cheeks were round as baked apples and her breasts were round as melons and her bottom was round as the prize pumpkins in the booths at the festival fair.

And I remembered that night at the dance as I fumbled about and tried to talk to the girl in the light blue gown, to get close to her, but ended up watching from afar as all the other boys and men laughed with her, and all the others danced with her, and all the others touched her arm or brushed against her warm young skin, and in my memories I again cursed my timidity.

But I also remembered I continued to watch and thrill at the sight of her and hope that the following year I would have greater courage and I would... And then suddenly the girl in the light blue gown was in front of me, smiling and holding out her hand and asking me to dance. And I remembered I lowered my eyes, and I was red with embarrassment, but I accepted her invitation.

I remembered she said she saw me watching her and she had never had anybody look at her that way and it excited her and she wanted to know if I really loved her the way my eyes caressed her and loved her.

I remembered that I said, yes, and she whispered, yes, and we danced closer, yes, and she touched me, yes, and my left hand rested at the top of her breasts, yes, and we left the dance floor and went to the animal barn and climbed up to the loft, yes, and she was not shy, yes, and so neither was I anymore, and we were both quickly naked and gasping in wonder at how beautiful we were to each other, yes, and she brought me inside her, yes, and we were not sweet or gentle or slow or patient, no, we pinched and squeezed so hard we left bruises on each other, and we bit and drew on each other until our bodies hurt with pleasure, yes, and we climaxed, yes, and we climaxed again, yes, and we climaxed once more, yes, before we fell exhausted onto the new-mown hay.

And when I dreamed I was at peace, and I forgot the things that had happened to me because I had familiar bodies and faces and voices to comfort me. And still La Bruja held me in her lap and stroked my fevered forehead...

And then, at the end of one of my dreams, on the 1,779th

Day of the Drought, my fever broke. I opened my eyes and saw La Bruja and Pritowski. I tried to sit up, but I was so weak I fell back onto La Bruja's lap.

And then I wept because I had been so happy in my dreams, and because I had been awakened and brought back to the land of the living dead.

Pritowski was the first to speak: "I was wrong. I did not think we would see you alive, Sandro."

But I ignored the doctor, and spoke to La Bruja. "Why have you brought me back? You should have let me go."

"Your time had not yet come," said La Bruja. "You have much to do before you find peace on the other side."

"But I have no desire left, not even my passion for revenge. I do not want anymore pain or suffering or the deaths of others."

"You still resist your fate," said La Bruja with a certain sense of wonder. "You have been given a great destiny. Why do you fight against it?"

I struggled to stay awake. I desperately wanted them to understand. I sighed when I thought about my dreams and what I had lost. "I was so much happier in my dreams. I did not choose this role you want to thrust upon me."

La Bruja knelt next to me and placed her hand on my cheek. "It is true you did not choose this path. You were chosen. The question remains: will you accept what has been given to you?"

As I thought about what she said, the smoke cleared from the room and I felt a little more clear-headed. My pain was mostly gone and my wounds were healed, although even La Bruja's magic could not undo all the damage the elements and Tokorotan's torture had wreaked upon me.

I answered La Bruja's question. "When I was asleep I...I remembered how simple my life once was. I would like to go back to that. I would like to go home."

La Bruja cackled in my ear. "You cannot go home again, dear Sandro. You have already come too far."

Pritowski smiled. "Maybe La Bruja is wrong, Sandro. Maybe you can go home, but how will you live with what has happened...and with what remains unfinished?"

"I am not up to it," I said. "If being The Chosen One means I am slowly torn apart, if living in this world means only suffering and despair, if revenge against the powers of evil means I must become evil myself, then what is gained? Maria never told me it would be like this. The Voice of the Shadowless Ones did not tell me how things would really be. Is all of this only for others? Am I to have nothing, not even the peace of death?"

"You ask questions we cannot answer, Sandro," said Pritowski. "We have all been born to make this happen that is all I know. Perhaps," he added, "Maria can answer your questions."

"Where is Maria?" I asked. "And why does she refuse to come to me?"

"I am not sure she has really abandoned you," said La Bruja. "I sent Pritowski to find her, but she is nowhere to be found."

"So," I said, "what do I do now?"

They looked at each other, then at me. Finally Pritowski spoke: "There is a rumor Maria is getting ready to open a new club with the financial backing of The Director of Finance. That is all I heard. No one has seen her. No one."

I felt a familiar anger stirring within me. "So Maria has returned to The Director of Finance? After everything?"

"It appears so," said Pritowski. "Or perhaps it is a ruse. We cannot know."

I looked down at my mutilated body. My missing fingers. The stumps where toes had been. The scars crisscrossing my chest where Tokorotan had carved his art into my flesh. "And what am I supposed to do like this? I am broken. I am nothing."

La Bruja grabbed my chin and forced me to look into her dark eyes. "You are not nothing. You are what you have always been, The Chosen One. The prophecy did not say The Chosen One would be whole. It did not say he would be beautiful. It only said he would come, and he would bring the rain."

"How?" I demanded. "How am I supposed to bring rain when I can barely stand?"

"That," said La Bruja, "is what you must discover. But know this: your mutilation is part of your power now, not separate from it. You have been broken and remade. You have died and returned. These are the marks of The Chosen One, Sandro. Not despite your suffering, but because of it."

I wanted to reject her words, but I could not. Deep within me, beneath the despair and the pain and the longing for my lost innocence, something stirred. Not hope exactly. Not yet. But perhaps the memory of hope. The ghost of what hope had once felt like.

"I need to see Maria," I said finally. "If she is truly opening a new club, then that is where I must go."

"You are not strong enough," said Pritowski.

"I will never be strong enough," I said. "But I will go anyway."

Chapter Fourteen: Forsaken

Do we ever really recover after being forsaken? We go on living...most of the time. But life, which had such vibrancy, becomes dull, hollow. Our emotions flatten out. Our voices lose their timbre. Our eyes glaze over. Desire fades...

And then the fire returns, first as fear, then revenge, then as a renewed, and perhaps even greater, passion to taste the fruits of living...to burn...to be consumed.

I decided I had to find Maria, even if she had abandoned me, even if she had gone over to the other side, although, in my heart, I did not believe she had done either of those things.

My plan was to station myself across the way from The Director of Finance's apartment. I pretended I was a beggar and since I already looked more wretched than most beggars, it was a very convincing disguise. Passersby even gave me money while doing everything possible to avoid eye contact.

By the end of the fifth day, I had given up hope of seeing either The Director of Finance or Maria. It was evening, and I was getting ready to leave when I saw them walking arm in arm down the street to the front door of the Central Governor's Building. They embraced and kissed and then Maria followed Madame Director into the building.

So, I decided to stay on the street. I covered myself with rags and copies of The Authoritarian so that I appeared to be a vagrant sleeping in the doorway which I guess I actually was. Anyway, I waited and waited. Finally, just before dawn, Maria left the building, alone, and walked across the street directly in front of me. Every fiber of my being wanted to reach out and touch her, to at least speak to her, but something, some sense of danger held me back. When she passed me she tossed a coin in my cup. Then she continued on down to the next road.

As soon as Maria turned the corner, The Director of Finance, in her mirrored glasses as always, also left her building, crossed the street exactly where Maria had passed right by me, did not drop a coin in my cup and carefully hugged the storefronts as she followed Maria's path. When she turned the same corner Maria had, I removed my rags and papers and warily followed Madame Director.

The three of us trailed each other for the next four or five hours. When Maria stopped to cross a street, The Director of Finance peered in a window as if she were shopping and I collapsed on the sidewalk. When Maria decided to eat pastry and drink coffee, Madame Director slipped into a corner grocery for fruit and I collapsed on the sidewalk. When Maria shopped in the bazaar, Madame Director stayed outside haggling with street vendors and I collapsed on the sidewalk.

Finally, Maria made her way into the Red Zone and entered a very old building covered with political slogans and torn, peeling revolutionary posters. Madame Director waited around outside for two hours, then she left. When darkness came and Maria remained inside the building, I decided it was safe for me to try to see her.

I entered as deliberately and cautiously as I could manage, continuing in my role as a vagrant looking for food and shelter in case I was stopped by someone I did not want to talk to.

The place was a mess. Garbage and refuse lined the hallways. The stench of rotting food and waste was everywhere. The rooms were deserted, their doors smashed and hanging from their hinges. The fixtures had been ripped and torn from the walls and ceilings.

I covered the first floor, and found nothing. On the second floor I found a closed door that was still intact, and I assumed Maria must be on the other side. However, after listening carefully for a few minutes and hearing no sound at all, I slowly opened the door and found the room completely empty just like all the others.

The third and final floor appeared as desolate as the first two, and I remember I had a sinking feeling that Maria had slipped out another entrance and I was wasting my time. Then, when I was ready to give up, I saw a flickering light under the door of the last room on the right. When I approached the door I also heard voices, so I entered the room next to the one with the light to see if I could hear whatever was going on through the walls.

Instead, I had some luck, or as things turned out, perhaps, misfortune. There was a shaft of light shining through a hole in the wall and I was able to see quite clearly into the other room. Maria was there, seated at a table, talking to two other figures. There were scattered papers all over the table. Maria and the other two were gesturing and arguing with each other. Finally, they seemed to resolve their argument, and all three relaxed in their chairs. One of the figures brought out a brown bottle and they all drank from it.

Whatever was in the bottle seemed to invigorate them. Maria stood and took off her jacket, then her shirt and her pants. I gasped. I could not help myself. I had forgotten how incredibly beautiful her body was. Those perfect breasts. The color of her skin. Her curly black hair and those long, long legs. She turned, and I could see that bottom, round and hard, sloping away from her long back.

The other two approached her. One began to kiss and squeeze her breasts. The other knelt and licked her back and her bottom. Maria raised her arms and folded her hands behind her head. I saw a look of pure pleasure in her eyes as the others' tongues explored her body. Her own tongue darted out, and she rolled it around her lips and breathed heavily through her nostrils.

Then the others disrobed. They were both men, in fact identical twins, and they had the most exquisite bodies I had seen in all my adventures. They were tall, slim yet broad-shouldered. They had long blond hair, piercing blue eyes, well-defined arms and legs. Their chests were virtually hairless with broad, firm muscles which tapered down to stomachs that were so tight the skin formed ridges that continued down to just above their blond hair. Their members were thick and smooth. Their foreskins had been removed, and the tips of their flesh had developed into large round heads with pronounced forms at the point where their foreskins would have been.

But it was their bottoms that made my blood race through my veins and my knees weak. They were so compact they did not move at all when they shifted but instead formed large concave dimples that accentuated their tight rounded form.

As I watched them lick Maria from head to toe, my own member grew hard. I felt my fluids rise, and one small drop escaped to wet my fingers.

Then one of them picked Maria up and placed her on the table. She knelt there while each of them took one of her breasts in his mouth and drew on and bit her nipples. She reached out and took a member in each hand and stroked them slowly, sensually back and forth, back and forth. One of them placed his fingers into her sex and pleasured her while the other spread her bottom apart and placed two wet fingers inside her entrance.

Then Maria was on her hands and knees, and I could see

her breasts sway as one twin entered her from behind and the other held his member up to her soft, wet mouth. She took them both into her. Their flesh glistened with their sweat and Maria's fluids which flowed out of her mouth and opening, then dripped onto the table.

Their tableau excited me so much I stroked myself even faster and moistened my hand for ease. I focused first on Maria's breasts, then on those two members moving in and out of her, and then on her face, then her breasts as they swung to and fro, to and fro, and then on the men's hard tight bottoms, then on Maria's face again as her eyes grew wide, and her breasts, her beautiful breasts seemed to wave in slow, slow motion beneath her vibrating body...

Then, at the very moment when both twins reached their climaxes, they removed their flesh and held them in their clenched fists while they sprayed their seed across Maria's bottom and into her thick curly hair while she pleasured herself and brought herself to a furious release.

But I could not release. My member shriveled in my hand when I felt my missing stone and remembered my missing fingers and I was overcome with shame. I saw perfection in those two men and realized how far my body had descended from that ideal. I was sick as I stumbled back from my opening, and realized I could never, ever face Maria again. So overwhelming was my self revulsion, I abandoned all caution and fled. I ran down the stairs, out of the building, out onto the street and into the waiting arms of the Central Authoritarian Guards who had surrounded the place where I had been.

"Who are you?" said the guard who held me.

"Let him go," said another guard. "Can you not see he is just a derelict. We have more important things to do."

"Wait," I said. "You must have the wrong place. There is no one in there."

But the guards ignored me. They were already streaming inside, and I knew there was no hope Maria would escape. In my panic, all I could think to do was to try to reach The Director of Finance and hope she could help Maria, so I ran toward the Central Governor's building.

When I arrived, I frantically tried to get inside. I banged on the door, I tried to break a window. Nothing worked.

Suddenly that street was also filled with Authoritarian Guards. They shoved me aside and broke down the front door. I crouched on the sidewalk fearing the worst. A few minutes later, the guards returned, dragging Madame Director with them.

"Madame Director!" I screamed. "They have captured Maria."

She turned and looked in my direction just as another vehicle pulled up next to us. To my horror, Tokorotan stepped out and walked over to Madame Director.

As the guards held The Director of Finance upright, Tokorotan struck her across the face. "No more of this," he shouted. "No more of this, you traitor! The Supreme Leader has declared all traitors must die." Then he drew his weapon and placed it against Madame Director's forehead.

"No," I yelled. "Nooooo..."

But Tokorotan was not to be stopped. He fired and destroyed Madame Director's head. Then he sauntered over to me.

"Your voice sounds familiar," he said. He reached down and grabbed my chin in his right hand. "Well, well," he chuckled, "The Chosen One." Then he struck me hard against the side of my head, and I passed out.

When I awakened, I knew immediately I was not on the 27th floor of the Central Police Station. Instead of unbearable noise, stifling heat and sickening odors, everything was completely silent...completely.

I heard an automatic door open and shut behind me, but when I turned and tried to get it to open, it remained firmly closed. When I ceased my struggling, an amplified voice spoke through a speaker at the end of a long hallway, "Welcome, Sandro."

I refused to answer.

"Come to the end of the hallway," the voice said.

When I reached the end of the hall, another panel opened and I was in a small room with a table on which there were blue prison clothes. The disembodied voice told me to change clothes. I complied without resistance.

When I was finished changing, another panel opened and stayed open until I passed through it. Then I walked through a series of opening and closing panels until I was in a tiny room that measured no more than two meters by four meters. There were no windows and no obvious doors. The walls were pale green. There was a small sink, no mirror, a tiny toilet bowl, a very narrow bed, and a single light in the ceiling that was always on.

I sat on the bed and waited. Nothing happened. I waited even longer. Still nothing happened. I felt like the walls were closing in on me, I was sweating and my hands were shaking. Then my whole body started to quiver and my mind was, to say the least, on very unstable ground.

A few hours later, a small panel opened and a cup of soup, two pieces of bread and a tin of water appeared. I ate the bread and soup and drank the water. They calmed me down a little. Then, when I put the empty containers back on the shelf, the panel opened again and they suddenly disappeared.

That routine kept up for the next few days, and at some point I realized it was going to continue for some time without my seeing or hearing anyone. My mind reeled at the thought. My palms were damp. My skin was cold and clammy.

On what I now guess must have been the tenth or eleventh day, I broke down completely and started to babble out loud. I do not even remember the things I said, but I am almost certain none of it made any sense. I began to pace constantly back and forth, back and forth. I felt like I did not sleep at all, although I probably did.

Finally, at one point, I remember...I was, yes, I was counting the number of paint speckles on the floor, when something inside my brain snapped. I remember I grew very, very tired, and after that, I think I gave up. I spent almost all my time on my bed. I did not exercise. I did not eat often. I did not pace about. I did not babble.

The solitary confinement was worse than Tokorotan's torture in some ways. Physical pain has an end: you pass out, you die, something gives way. But this endless silence, this complete isolation, this slow erosion of self had no limit. I began to forget what my own voice sounded like. I began to doubt whether I had ever existed outside this green box. Maria, Alexander, Mariann, my parents, the girl at the festival, had they been real or merely dreams I had invented to comfort myself?

I tried to hold onto memories but they slipped away through my mutilated fingers. I tried to remember Maria's face but could only see the twins' perfect bodies. I tried to remember my home but could only see this green room. I tried to remember my name but it sounded foreign, like a word from a language I had never spoken.

Sometimes I wondered if this was what death was like. Not darkness, but endless pale green light. Not silence exactly, but the absence of all human sound. Not pain, but the absence of all feeling. Perhaps I had died already and this was my eternity.

Other times I convinced myself this was all a test. The Chosen

One had to pass through ultimate isolation to achieve ultimate unity with the people. I had to lose myself completely in order to find my true purpose. But these thoughts felt hollow, like stories I was telling myself to avoid the truth: I was simply a broken man in a green box, and I would remain here until I stopped being anything at all.

I counted the meals. Then I lost count. I again counted the paint speckles. Then I lost interest. I counted my breaths. Then I stopped caring. Time became meaningless. Had I been there days? Weeks? Months? Years? There was no way to know. The light never changed. The routine never varied. Nothing ever happened except the appearance and disappearance of food through the small panel.

And slowly, very slowly, I felt myself dissolving. Not dying, that would have been too merciful. Just...dissolving. Becoming less. Becoming nothing. The green walls absorbed me bit by bit until I was no longer certain where I ended and they began.

Finally, after six months in solitary, and on the 1,977th Day of the Drought, I was removed from my cell and brought to trial before the Central Supreme Court.

Chapter Fifteen: Justice

Justice is blind. It is blind, not because it wears a blindfold against prejudice; it is blind because it cannot see the truth.

Since none of us can ever really know the truth, then of course there can never be such a thing as justice. But we live together so that we can be protected from each other. And we feel protected because we assume the bad people are going to get their comeuppance. We will even let governments commit murder, theft and mayhem if we feel they nonetheless provide redress against our neighbors.

So, we go about making up various forms of distributing rewards and punishments, and we call our chosen forms of distribution, 'justice.' We even argue about which distribution system is more just. But there is no justice because there is no truth. That is why justice is blind.

Chief Justice Eleanora could not use the excuse that she was blind. Not only was her vision perfect, she knew what was going on, and there was no question in her mind about whether I was guilty or innocent. "Still," as she said to me in her chambers, "we must go through this process of making your obvious innocence appear to be incontrovertible proof of your guilt."

Eleanora wore a white powder wig and sat behind her bench in a high backed brown leather chair. She often played with her gavel during my trial, and she had an unconscious habit of running her fingers back and forth on the handle as if she were pleasuring a very stiff young man. She also wore long black robes with full sleeves and black shoes with brass buckles. As I was later to discover during a discussion in her chambers, under her robes she wore black stockings, a red garter belt, red silk undergarments and a red lace covering for her breasts.

It was never clear to me what the charges against me were. It did not seem to matter. Chief Justice Eleanora, Central Prosecuting Attorney Rebecca and Public Defender Mariella knew their lines well enough.

"There is no question the defendant was, on the night in question, engaged in activity that can only be called seditious," asserted Prosecuting Attorney Rebecca.

Public Defender Mariella jumped to her feet. "I object, there is no evidence, to say nothing of proof, that such behavior can be called seditious."

"An interesting question," Chief Justice Eleanora said as she nodded sagely, "we agree the defendant was there on the day in question, acting in a certain manner...but was that in fact seditious behavior according to the Code of Central Law?"

"I assert, Madam Justice, that the applicable code was Law 4765, chapter 96, subsection 23a," said Prosecuting Attorney Rebecca.

"And I believe we should be dealing with Central Law 26934, chapter 820, subsection 2169c.56d," said my lawyer.

"I cannot really say either of you are correct," said Chief Justice Eleanora. "I am more inclined to think we should proceed as if the relevant code is Central Law 67, chapter 263967, subsection 2g.4k."

They went on and on and on like that. I usually fell asleep until they made the guard who always sat next to me poke me in the ribs. Then I was forced to stay awake through another meaningless exchange. The codes they cited were so obscure, so ancient, that I suspected they were simply inventing them.

Perhaps there was a Central Law 67, chapter 263967, subsection 2g.4k. Perhaps there was not. It made no difference. The performance was what mattered, not the substance.

When we broke to discuss matters in the Chief Justice's chambers things were a bit more interesting. The three of them sat in large lounge chairs arranged in a semi-circle around a glass topped coffee table. I was told to sit on a straight-backed chair across the room, facing Justice Eleanora, while they discussed my case.

My defense lawyer, Mariella, usually opened the discussion by arguing that although I was clearly guilty, there were mitigating factors which should limit my ultimate sentence. Her favorite tactic was to point at me across the room, describe me as pathetic, detail my wounds and disfigurements and ask for the minimum sentence. Obviously not a very comforting defense.

Justice Eleanora would agree I was pathetic, but argue that the state must not only be protected, I must also become an example for those who would act against it. The Chief Justice further argued that it made no difference whether I was a dangerous criminal or not. Once the state had declared I was, then the state's obligation was to impose the proper punishment.

Rebecca was the toughest on me. She would not even agree I was pathetic. She described my long history of activities against the Central Authorities, going all the way back to my relationship with a certain fortune teller who ran an anti-authoritarian cell out of storefront number 716 and wrote secret tracts which fed popular resentment against the Central Authorities, a fact which if true, I never knew. She felt my condition was only a ruse to gain sympathy, and that I should receive the obvious punishment imposed on those who would overthrow the state: death. By that point, I was so destroyed by what I had been through, I was inclined to agree with her, and I always supported her arguments on the occasions when they asked me to speak.

But they certainly did not ask me to speak very often. In fact they were not interested in me at all. I was only the pretext for them to discuss the latest political gossip and carry on their incessant affairs.

In the courtroom, Mariella and Rebecca also wore the long black robes mandated for all those appearing before the Chief Justice on official business, although they were not forced to wear wigs. However, the Chief Justice's private chambers were another matter.

Mariella was a strikingly handsome brunette. She had blue eyes, tinted, wire framed glasses and an easy, infectious smile which had the effect of disarming people who might otherwise be hostile to her defense of common criminals and traitors. She wore white lace coverings that cradled her magnificent breasts, and she was partial to tiny little white garments that just covered the thin strip of dark hair she did not shave.

Rebecca was a brown-eyed blond. She was rather stout, but her figure was in proportion to her size. Under her robes she was a large, strong, fleshy woman who did not like restraining garments. She preferred simple coverings and garter belts. Her face was pleasant but plain, even direct. She was not given to great emotion. She relied on her strength and power.

The three of them finally decided on my sentence in Eleanora's chambers two days before the results were formally announced in open court. We were all sitting in our usual places when Justice Eleanora announced the Central Authorities had told her it was time to reach a verdict. "So," she sighed, "what shall we do?"

"Well," said Public Defender Mariella, "in light of his lengthy pretrial incarceration, as well as his two difficult interrogations, I would say a light sentence, say five years, would be appropriate." She opened her robe to her waist and let the other two glimpse the delights that awaited them if they agreed with her.

Prosecuting Attorney Rebecca pretended not to notice. "Sandro is a traitor and a murderer. He has incited others to violence against the state. He is a pretender to leadership in our most sacred institutions. He must die." She pulled back the flowing arms of her own gown and flexed her powerful muscles to remind the others that she was dominant.

Chief Justice Eleanora leaned back in her chair and spread her legs so her robe hung down either side of her body and her scarlet garters and garments were exposed. Then she raised her arms, leaned back and not very accidentally allowed the top of her robe to fall open and reveal her red lace covering. Both Mariella and Rebecca realized the contest was about to begin in earnest. Although their approaches were different, they both showed intense interest as they contemplated their individual strategies.

Mariella was the first to present her final arguments. She moved gracefully as she walked over to Eleanora and kissed her on the lips. Then she moved her mouth a few centimeters from Eleanora's mouth and they touched the tips of each other's tongues. Eleanora groaned and let her body relax ever more deeply into her chair. Mariella licked the justice's neck, nibbled on her ears, kissed her mouth and moved down to release her covering.

Once Mariella had freed the chief justice's breasts, she pulled her own white lacy covering up around her neck which exposed her two very large, but firm, very rounded breasts. That made Eleanora sigh. Mariella pinched her own nipples to make them hard. Then she rubbed her nipples against the justice's nipples. The judge closed her eyes and moaned.

Next, Mariella lowered her dark red lips onto Eleanora's breasts and drew on them very sweetly. Then she positioned her leg between the justice's thighs and rubbed her soft white skin up against Eleanora's center.

And so she rubbed and drew on and drew on and rubbed until the judge could take no more. Eleanora's hips vibrated with spastic convulsions as she rubbed back and forth on Mariella's leg. Then she tensed, groaned, gave one tremendous push against Mariella and collapsed completely into her chair.

Rebecca had watched this performance objectively, analytically. When she sensed the Chief Justice had recovered, she went down on her knees and went directly for Eleanora's dripping sex. As her tongue slowly caressed Eleanora's center, she placed her hands on the judge's bottom and lifted it into the air so she could manipulate Eleanora's movements while she licked and drew on her.

The Chief Justice's eyes bulged and she reached up to pinch and pull on her own nipples while Rebecca took care of the rest of her. Rebecca's strength was unbelievable. She kept lifting the chief justice's body higher and higher, each time increasing the pressure and pleasure without Eleanora needing to do anything. Rebecca moved the judge's hips faster and faster while her tongue moved more and more quickly, drawing on and kissing and kissing and drawing on until Eleanora could not take anymore and she literally exploded off the chair and fell into a quivering heap on the floor.

Rebecca appeared triumphant. I was also delighted, certain I had finally achieved my death sentence and this Chosen One business was finally over with. But Mariella had other ideas.

She crept up behind Rebecca and began to rub her breasts against Rebecca's back. Then she leaned over and whispered into Rebecca's ear. Then she reached around and pinched the Central Prosecutor's nipples while she continued to squirm and move her body against Rebecca's back and bottom. I was certain the prosecutor would not be swayed by my lawyer's advances. I held my breath in anticipation of Rebecca's angry response, but instead, the woman sighed, turned and put her mouth onto Mariella's mouth.

Mariella was not about to lose her advantage. She leaned back and pulled Rebecca on top of her without once taking her mouth away from the prosecutor's mouth or her fingers from the prosecutor's nipples. Then, when she was certain she would have her way, she slid her mouth down Rebecca's neck and shoulders until she could get her lips onto the prosecutor's breasts. Then, instead of licking them, she began to bite them. Meanwhile she moved her hands behind Rebecca and began to strike the Central Prosecutor's bottom.

The response was everything Mariella could have hoped for. Rebecca's breath came in great gasps. Her eyes were half closed and her hips began to move against Mariella's body. Mariella continued her downward movement until her mouth was on Rebecca's sex and her tongue was moving across the prosecutor's center. Then she executed a beautiful reversal by slipping out from under Rebecca, twisting onto her knees facing Rebecca's bottom, and then biting the prosecutor's behind while she slowly worked her fist up into Rebecca's opening.

That was it. The Central Prosecuting Attorney went wild. She whimpered and screamed and cried out. She shook and moved across the floor. She begged Mariella not to stop.

Mariella simply said, "No death penalty. Life imprisonment."

"Yes," said Rebecca, "Oh yes, yes, yes, anything. Just do not stop. Please, please do not stop."

Mariella looked across at Chief Justice Eleanora who had been watching the two lawyers and was furiously pleasuring herself with her gavel. Chief Justice Eleanora nodded her agreement with the arrangement, and so, as they all climaxed together, my fate was sealed in that tangle of writhing bodies.

I sat there in my straight-backed chair, watching the three women who held my life in their hands collapse in exhaustion on the floor of the Chief Justice's chambers. The absurdity of it all was not lost on me. My fate, whether I would live or die, had been decided not by evidence or law or even political necessity, but by which woman could bring the others to greater pleasure.

And I realized that this too was part of being The Chosen One. Not just torture and mutilation and solitary confinement, but this: bearing witness to the grotesque theater of power. Watching as those who held authority revealed themselves to be nothing more than flesh seeking pleasure, bodies seeking release, humans playing dress-up in black robes and pretending their desires were principles.

The trial itself continued for another month after that evening. Each day, the three women performed their roles with practiced precision. Rebecca would cite obscure laws and demand death. Mariella would point at my pathetic form and plead for mercy. Eleanora would nod sagely and postpone her decision. And each evening, in the privacy of the chambers, they would negotiate my sentence again through their elaborate rituals, always reaching the same conclusion that had been decided that first night.

I learned not to hope. Hope was dangerous. Hope suggested that reason or mercy or justice might prevail. But I had seen behind the curtain. I knew that justice was not blind. It was simply distracted, easily swayed by the promise of pleasure, negotiable in the currency of flesh.

Sometimes, during the endless legal arguments, I would think about Maria. Was she somewhere in this same building, facing her own absurd trial? Or had they simply executed her immediately, without bothering with the theater of justice? I would never know. They would not tell me, and I could not ask without revealing that I cared, without giving them one more thing to take from me.

On the final day, Chief Justice Eleanora stood in her white wig and black robes and pronounced my sentence with great solemnity: "Sandro, you have been found guilty of sedition, treason, and conspiracy to overthrow the state. The court has considered all the evidence and all the arguments. Taking into account your cooperation and your obvious suffering, the court sentences you to life imprisonment in the Central Penitentiary. May the state have mercy on your soul."

The courtroom erupted. Some cheered that The Chosen One would rot forever in prison. Others wept that I had not been executed and martyred. I felt nothing. I simply stood and allowed the guards to take me away.

As they led me out, I caught one last glimpse of the three women. They were already gathering their papers, preparing for their next case, their next performance. My life had been decided between their legs, and now it was over. They would go home to their lovers or their meals or whatever occupied them when they were not playing at justice. And I would go to my cell.

And on the 2,067th Day of the Drought, I began my life sentence in the Central Penitentiary.

Chapter Sixteen: Rape

Rape is violence. Rape has nothing to do with desire. Desire is pleasure. Violence is pain. Desire is connection. Violence is anguish. Desire is joy. Violence is suffering. Yet, violence definitely involves the body. There must be a component of physical connection that is hostile, angry and abusive. Otherwise, the body would not work as a weapon. Pain and humiliation. Humiliation and pain.

I know for sure that Strucker thought such questions were not worth considering. He was a prisoner in the Central Penitentiary, a killer who found satisfaction in the pain and death he caused others: He murdered his father when he was eleven and left the mutilated body to rot among the chaparral on a sun bleached hillside; at thirteen he killed his little brother by suffocation when he tied a bag around the child's head; he burned his mother and his sisters while he destroyed his house when he was seventeen. As an adult, he had killed three other adults outside the prison walls and another four inside. He proudly proclaimed he liked killing better each time he did it.

The Central Authorities condemned Strucker's murders, but they never discussed putting him to death. It did not take me more than a few days in the Central Penitentiary to understand why, Strucker was very useful to them. In a place filled with violent men, Strucker, the most violent of all men, helped keep the peace. And if inconvenient or embarrassing prisoners accidentally got in his way and, as a result, disappeared, then so much the better.

I first saw Strucker in the yard on my second day inside. In truth, I would not have noticed him at all were it not for the deference the other prisoners paid him. Like many truly evil men, Strucker was the perfection of banality. He was not imposing. He was not tall. He was not ugly. He did not have markings all over his body or scars across his face. His hair was not unusually short or long. He wore standard issue prison clothes which he had not altered in any way.

He was so ordinary I did not appreciate his explosive power until the second time I saw him. I was in the dining hall, and Strucker was sitting at a table a few meters away. He was in a deep discussion with two other inmates when a hapless prisoner accidentally tripped and dropped his tray at Strucker's feet. Strucker did not even stop his conversation as he calmly stood up and noticed food on his shoes. For a brief second, his eyes grew very tiny and flashed crystal hatred. He picked up the fallen prisoner's fork and very deliberately pushed it through the man's cheek. Then he sat back down and resumed his conversation as if nothing had happened.

Two days after the incident in the dining hall, I was in the exercise area on the roof. I was still too weak and dispirited to actually do any exercise, but I always lingered on the roof as long as I possibly could because lying in the hot sun was the only comfort my broken, twisted body ever had. When Strucker approached me, I must have fallen asleep in the heat.

I was daydreaming, mulling over different plans to make contact with Maria in the prison's women's wing, when I heard a flat voice say, "Well, if it is not the new cripple."

I opened my eyes and found Strucker's body was a looming black outline, backlit by the sun's bright light. He opened his pants and pulled out a member as unremarkable and uninteresting as the rest of him.

His dull, soft flesh dangling in front of my face certainly

did not excite me. I closed my eyes and said, "Could you please move out of the sunlight?"

My rejection of him, or more accurately, my boredom with him, enraged Strucker. With one hand he lifted me off the bench. Then he grabbed my shoulders and shook me violently. I was, to him, an insignificant, broken puppet. His eyes narrowed, and that look I had seen before in the dining hall flickered across his face. He stripped off my shirt and tore it to shreds.

As his anger intensified, Strucker's member grew erect. He pulled my prison uniform down to my ankles, and I offered no further resistance. In fact I bent over and presented myself in total surrender and resignation. I waited...and waited, but nothing happened. After a few seconds, I realized his aggressive behavior had stopped. I turned around and saw that he was soft again. The fire was also gone from his eyes. "Resist me," he whispered, "Resist me...Fight me...Struggle with me."

He was pathetic.

"To the depths with you," I said, "Just finish the job."

I could feel his eyes on me. His confusion hung in the air; he simply could not understand. "You are not afraid to die?" he said in wonder.

"No, I am not," I said.

"And they told me people on the outside were calling you The Chosen One," he said. "But, you are weak, without courage, submissive, like a...like a...a woman."

I ignored him.

"Do you not understand I can do what I want with you? No one cares," he said, but an uncertain bragging had crept into his voice.

"Then stop talking and do it," I said.

His eyes flickered, but then they focused on my groin and he was again distracted. He reached over, grabbed my member and stared at it. "The Inquisitor's work?"

When I did not answer, he stood up, stepped back and looked at the rest of my body. "And your nipple. The cuts. Your missing teeth. Tokorotan?"

Again, I did not answer him.

He turned me around, and I felt his hands on my bottom, my back, my shoulders. "Beautiful," he whispered, "they both really do beautiful work. If only I had their tools, their work space..." Then he sighed and that slight edge of fear slithered back into his voice. "So little time. So little time left...to do my work." Then he abruptly turned me back around to face him. His eyes flashed again and I remember thinking, finally he is going to kill me. I was neither happy nor sad, only ready.

Instead he slammed his fist into my mouth so hard he broke my jaw. The pain was terrible, but somehow I prepared myself for more. I stared into the sun and focused on the light.

But the next blow never came. Strucker stood there for a few moments. Then he grunted. "Since you do not care if you die," he said, "then you will...die. But not how you think. Not easily, the way you want it. I have got a...a special surprise...for you." He discharged saliva on the ground next to me. "Chosen One...foolish idiot. If anyone is, I am The Chosen One, yeah, chosen to administer vengeance, to render judgment, to cleanse, yes, to cleanse...to...clean...up...this...this world from crippled, disgusting vermin like yourself." Then his rambling discourse broke off into mumblings I could not understand. As he walked away, he added. "You will be chosen all right because I will choose you." He laughed at his own private joke. "I will choose you for a very, very special occasion."

After that incident and a few more days in the infirmary, my prison time faded into an endless waiting game. I kept to myself, and did not talk to anyone. I watched and waited, always seeking an opportunity to get any information I could about the women's wing, always watching the women when they exercised or were marched through the yard, hoping for a glimpse of Maria, hoping she was still alive.

One day I was certain I saw her hugging the gray stone wall beneath one of the guard towers along the far side of the yard. My excitement was intense and my heart was pounding, but when I looked again, she had disappeared...or I never really saw her in the first place. But I continued my vigil. I waited...

My lawyer, Mariella, sent me a note. She said we had no chance of winning an appeal, but I should keep my spirits up while she tried a clemency persuasion. I waited. Weeks passed. Then months. I waited.

And so one night they came for me as they always do, in the middle of the night, when I was asleep. By the time I was aware of what was going on, there were already two guards in my cell. One of them held me down while the other tore off my pants. "My God," he said, "what does Strucker want with this mutilated, crippled, wretched creature."

"Just shut up and do your work," the other one said. After that, they did not talk while they removed every last piece of my clothes. Then they dragged me, naked, from my cell. I saw no point in resisting, and I did not raise even a murmur of protest.

We stopped at the prison's unused and deserted shower room, and they took me inside. I was amazed when they turned one of the faucets and water came out. The taller guard threw me a bar of soap. "Wash," he said as if there were nothing particularly strange about that request.

I figured if I was going to die, it would be pleasant to do so with a clean body, so I stood under the flow and let the water run over me while I lathered soap all over. The water felt wonderful, and I wanted to stay forever, but the guards shut off the stream after a few minutes. Then the shorter guard reached into a bag he had been carrying, and pulled out a white garment which he told me to put on, immediately. It was only when I held the clothes up in front of me that I realized it was a wedding dress.

At first I was stunned and more than a little confused, but the guards were hurrying me along so I put the dress on as best I could. Then they gave me a veil and a pair of white high-heeled shoes. The shoes actually fit.

The guards laughed when they observed the strange apparition they had helped create. "And what entertainment are we going to have now?" I asked.

"We are going to a wedding," was all they would say. They each grabbed an arm and walked me down the empty corridors toward the prison chapel.

When we opened the doors to the chapel, my first sensation was one of intense, almost painful, brightness because the chapel was filled with burning candles and strobe lights. My second impression was that I would suffocate in the stifling unbearable heat from the lights and the large room full of bodies. My third overpowering impression was of the loud buzz, the steady humming noise created by the whispers and murmuring of the prisoners.

It seemed to me that all the inmates from the men's wing were jammed into that chapel, and they probably were. I noticed everyone was staring at me in my white wedding gown, and I was so embarrassed I pulled the old, torn veil over my face to avoid their looks, but then they all clapped as if I had done the proper thing. The organist played the wedding march, and I began my slow progression down the aisle toward the altar. When I reached the altar, Strucker, dressed in formal clothes walked over and stood next to me. Then the prison chaplain left the sanctuary and stood in front of us.

"Brothers, we are gathered here today..." he intoned, and I

realized we really were going to celebrate an elaborate mockery of the traditional wedding ceremony.

As the chaplain continued with the ancient rites of matrimony, my mind started to wander back to weddings I had attended as a child. The joyful ceremonies on the green plains, with tables laden with food and musicians playing through the night. I remembered my cousin's wedding, how she had looked so beautiful in white, how everyone had danced until dawn. I remembered thinking that someday I too would stand at an altar with someone I loved, in front of people who cared for us.

And now here I was, in a white dress, at an altar, surrounded by witnesses. A perfect mockery of everything a wedding was supposed to be. A ceremony of violation instead of union. A ritual of death instead of life.

Suddenly, I felt Strucker's elbow in my ribs. He leaned over, and said, "Well, do you?"

I looked at him, but I did not understand. Then he bent his head toward the chaplain. I looked at the chaplain who repeated his question, "Do you, Sandro, take Strucker to be your lawfully wedded husband, for richer or poorer, in sickness and health, until death do you part?"

Something about "until death do you part" made me chuckle, but the entire affair seemed so absurd I saw no harm in answering, "Yes." All the prisoners clapped and cheered.

Then the chaplain said a few other words before I heard him say, "Strucker, you may now take the bride."

Strucker struck me and knocked me to the ground. His best man, also in formal clothes, held me down with my knees under my stomach so my bottom stuck up in the air. Then someone, probably Strucker, pulled my wedding dress up over my buttocks. Again there was clapping and cheering from the prisoners.

Suddenly a large, cold, rough metal object was forced into my body. Pain shot along my nerve endings, and I thought for a moment I was again being tortured with high voltage electricity. I cried out even though I had promised myself I would not do that. Meanwhile the rough metal object was being manipulated in and out of my entrance. I felt my skin tearing. I felt the blood running down my legs. The prisoners were yelling like wolves catching the scent of raw meat. I was weeping and hoping I would go into shock, but I did not.

Then the metal object was removed, and I felt Strucker's member inside my body. The prisoners groaned. Strucker started his movements, pushing back and forth, faster and faster. Each time he pushed into me, the entire prison population groaned in unison.

Their exhortations excited Strucker, and he began to shout and yell as he struck himself against my bottom. Finally his movements were so frenzied I knew he was getting ready to release. That was when I also realized the words he was shouting in time with each thrust, "Die, die, die, die, die, die, yes, oh yes, yes, die, die, die, die, die, die, die, yes, god, yes, die, die, die, die!"

And then, on the 2,437th Day of the Drought, Strucker's seed entered me and mixed with my blood.

I lay there on the chapel floor in my torn wedding dress, my body broken once more, my spirit descending into a darkness I had not known existed. The prisoners filed out slowly, their entertainment concluded. The guards came and dragged me back to my cell, throwing me onto the concrete floor like refuse.

I did not move for days. They brought food, but I did not eat. They brought water, but I did not drink. I simply lay there, feeling the pain in my body transform into something else, not acceptance, but a kind of emptiness. A void where hope or rage or even despair might otherwise have been.

And yet, even in that void, something stirred. Not The Chosen One, that myth had died long ago. But perhaps something more fundamental. The simple animal will to continue. To witness. To endure.

Because I understood now what I had not understood before. This too was part of the prophecy. Not one of the glorious parts, not the triumph or the rain or the redemption. But this: the complete destruction of Sandro, so that something else might eventually emerge. The Chosen One could not be born from strength. He had to be born from absolute annihilation.

La Bruja had been right. My mutilation was my power. And now, with this final degradation, the transformation was nearly complete.

I was no longer the young man who had left the green plains. I was no longer the lover who had followed Maria. I was no longer even the tortured prisoner who had stumbled through the desert. I was something new. Something forged in pain and humiliation and absolute powerlessness.

What that something was, I did not yet know. But I would discover it soon enough.

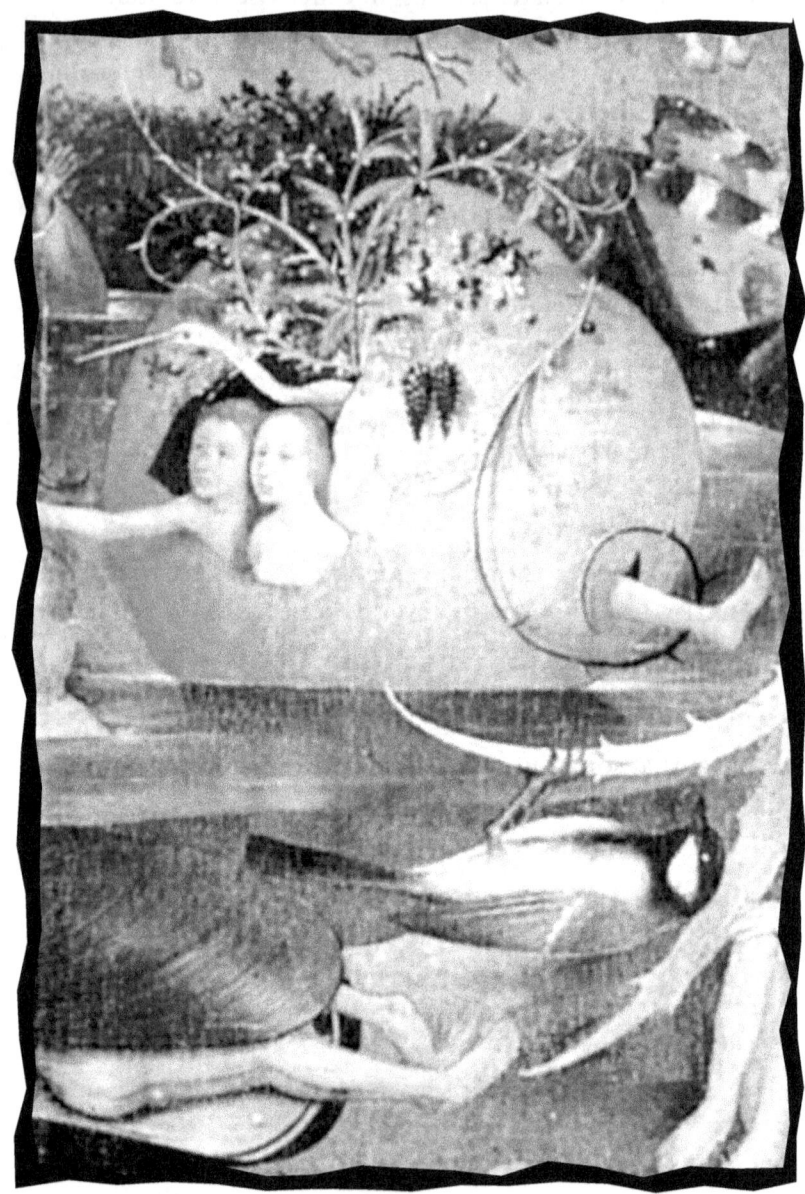

Chapter Seventeen: Love

Love is always found in the strangest of places. We can seek love among friends, where we work, in our neighborhoods, or at school, where we play, in the restaurants where we eat. All to no avail. No matter how perfect the place, how right the atmosphere, how compatible the people, our search often comes to naught.

Then, as we sadly walk away from one of those perfect situations with the perfect person, we will bump into someone on the street, look into their eyes and be completely smitten. Or we will end up in the most unlikely part of town and see someone... Or we will be at a party having a miserable time with people we cannot stand when someone enters the room...

After Strucker's violence, I certainly never thought I would fall in love, particularly in prison, particularly with a man, particularly with a man like Spider. But, after the rest of the prisoners had enjoyed my humiliation and left the chapel, Spider was the only one who held me and comforted me. What is more, he was the only one who would share a cell with me after I had been released from the infirmary.

Spider was a tall man with big brown eyes and a full head of curly black hair. He had light brown, almost hairless skin, and well defined arms and legs from working out on heavy weights and running in place for hours at a time. His teeth were wide and white, his chest was large and firm, his bottom was hard and round and his member was substantial and beautiful. But the most incredible thing about him was the blue and gold spider he had tattooed on his chest.

The spider sat on a finely detailed web that ran from his left shoulder across his neck line to his right shoulder, down to his navel and back over to his left hip. The threads of the web were portrayed so delicately, that at first I did not believe it could be a tattoo.

Still, the web was nothing compared to the spider itself. It sat on his chest, just above his left nipple and was the size of a large walnut. The legs and the body were rendered in florescent cobalt blue, while the head and the spinnerets were done in genuine, brilliant gold. Each time he breathed, the spider moved, the spinnerets spun, and the web shimmered.

But I did not see the tattoo the first time I met Spider. I did not really see anything at all. As I lay there on the floor in a pool of my own blood and Strucker's seed, Spider leaned over me and wrapped a blanket around my naked bleeding body, lifted me off the floor and carried me to the infirmary where, as it turned out, no one would have anything to do with me. It was Spider who washed me and applied ointment to my wounds. It was Spider who made up a bed with clean sheets, and it was Spider who kissed me when he left my room.

The next morning a nurse came by with a breakfast tray which she left on a table near my bed. No one else came to see me except to leave or pick up food trays. No one examined me. No one touched me in any way. That evening it was again Spider who tended my wounds and cared for me and cleaned things.

I asked him why no one had been by to see me, and why the staff was avoiding me. "Well, there is really no need for them to see you," he said. "I mean, you know Strucker was pretty rough on you, but your wounds will heal, Sandro. Meanwhile, you have me to take care of you." Then he smiled and showed the twinkle in his eye and his white teeth and everything seemed to be all right although I suppose I knew even then that it was not really.

I must have stayed in the infirmary for three, maybe four days. On the morning of the fourth day, Spider came to see me very early, even before the sun came up. He told me I could leave with him, and when I gathered my few belongings and followed him out the door, no one stopped me or questioned me.

Spider took me to his cell and told me I could live with him. I said that would be fine as long as the guards would let us be together. Well, little did I know that they would not only let us live together, in fact, when it was time for us to leave and eat breakfast in the dining hall, a guard instead delivered two food trays to our cell. That really did confuse me, and I was very suspicious. "You must be a very special prisoner," I said.

"Yeah," he said. "I guess I am." An ironic smile crossed his lips, but at that point he did not volunteer any more information and I did not pursue it.

That afternoon he asked if I wanted to go up on the roof while he worked out on his weights. I said I would like to be in the sunshine although I did not want to be around the other prisoners after what had happened to me. But my fears were groundless. When we got to the roof, no one else was there.

"Wait a minute," I said, "this is not by chance, Spider. What is happening?"

"They have always allowed me to work out alone," was his only answer. "You can come up here with me any time you want and read or just lay in the sun if you wish."

"All right," I said, "I will. Yes, I...will..." But I did have mixed emotions. On the one hand, if I was going to be in prison, it was certainly a lot easier not have to deal with the other prisoners, especially after what I had been through and when I looked as terrible as I did. On the other hand, something was obviously strange about Spider's life, about the authorities' willingness to let him live apart from the rest of the population and their acceptance, even eagerness to have me be with him.

So, I sat in the sun and watched Spider lift and stretch and run in place. It was actually very exciting because he was bare chested and wore very brief baggy shorts. His skin seemed particularly rich and smooth as I watched his muscles ripple along his forearms and biceps, and up and down his calves and thighs. When he was so concentrated and focused like that, I could not imagine a more complete image of physical perfection. When I tried to remember if I had ever seen him before, I realized I had not before that night he picked me up from the chapel floor. Instead of reading, I spent most of my time speculating: Who was he? What had he done to get himself put in prison? And why was he separated from the other prisoners?

The more I tried to figure things out, the more confused I became. After a while, I dozed off. There did not seem to be any meaningful answers to my labyrinth of questions, and the best course for me to follow was to accept my chance to rest and enjoy whatever relative good fortune came my way.

A few nights later, after dinner, Spider and I were talking and I suddenly found myself telling him my entire story: the truth as I saw it, exactly as it happened. When I looked at him to see his reaction to what I told him, I noticed he was crying. When I asked him why, he said he never dreamed he would actually meet The Chosen One.

That was the only time I ever lost my temper and became angry with Spider. I cursed him up and down and screamed, "I am not The Chosen One! Is that not obvious? I was not...am not...and will not be!"

But he just smiled his beautiful smile, reached under his bed, pulled out a pamphlet from the Cathedral of The Living

Truth and said, "It is written: He will deny from whence he came or what path he taketh because he knoweth not his purpose although he shall, nonetheless, in fulfilling his destiny rescue us from sin, pestilence and drought. So..."

I could tell even the possibility I might be The Chosen One meant a great deal to him, and, because he had been so good to me, I decided to let him believe whatever he wanted to believe. But then he knelt at my feet and began to kiss my toes. I was, to say the least, extremely uncomfortable to have that exquisite creature pay homage to me, to my totally shattered and ravaged body. "No," I said, "Stop."

When he would not, I said, "I command you to stop." He looked up at me so sadly with those big, brown eyes, and started to speak, but I placed my finger on his lips. "It is I who should pay homage to you," I said. He was startled, but I did not let him think about what I had said. I held out my hand and motioned for him to sit on the bed next to me. When he did, I slipped off his shirt, rested my head on his chest and kissed his nipple just below the tattooed spider.

I was excited to see the tattoo close up like that. I lightly traced the intricate design of the web with my little finger. Spider sighed and closed his eyes. I could see his nipples were hard and I knew he was stimulated by my touch. Then I brushed my fingers across the golden-headed creature itself. Spider moaned, and his stomach and chest muscles rapidly expanded and contracted.

I gently pushed him back onto his bed, and as he lay there, breathing heavily, I licked along every strand of the blue spider's web and left a light trail of moisture which glistened like the dew on a silk web in an early morning field back on the Great Plains. When I moved my tongue back and forth on the spider itself, Spider flexed his chest muscles so powerfully the tattooed spider seemed to be crawling across his chest.

As his excitement reached a fever pitch, I undid his pants and pulled them down to reveal his wonderful long member. As I held it in my hand and admired it like the extraordinary work of art that it was, I noticed the veins that ran along the shaft when it was filled with Spider's blood. When I pulled back his covering, the tip was smooth, moist, inviting. I took him into my mouth and softly drew on his rigid flesh with my toothless gums.

Spider almost immediately released inside my mouth, but rather than enjoy his pleasure, he became very upset, weeping that he had blasphemed, that he was damned, that his life was meaningless. As we lay there together on his bed, I gently cradled his head in my arms and told him it was not a sin to love, and physical pleasure was not evil in the world of The Chosen One. He took comfort from my words and pressed close against me, a difficult trick for one so large and powerful.

And so I continued to soothe him, and when I felt his member grow hard against my stomach, I again kissed his chest and played with the spider and when he was ready, drew on his beautiful flesh. The second time he did not release so quickly or so easily, and our joy lasted a very long time.

After that evening, Spider and I were inseparable. In his eyes I had the power and experience to make him feel he was living with a god; and for me, just being with him made me feel alive again despite all my injuries and mutilations. We ate together, we walked together, we talked together, we slept together.

In fact it was Spider who finally was able to make contact with the women's wing to find out if there was any news about Maria.

The separate men's and women's wings were two entirely different buildings and the only common area was the yard. Over the years, the prisoners had developed an elaborate system of hand signals to communicate with each other from the windows of their wing when one or the other group was in the yard. Unfortunately, Spider was not very adept at communicating that way since he was virtually a hermit. Worse, he had no friends in either prison who could vouch for him, so it took him a long time to make contact with someone who could give us any news.

After a couple of months we finally found out that Maria was in the prison, that she was being held in maximum security solitary confinement on the floor where they kept those prisoners scheduled for execution. That meant it was definitely not Maria I had seen in the yard, and, in fact, very few of the women prisoners had ever seen her or talked to her. She was alive, however, and as far as anyone knew, healthy.

The news about Maria stirred complex feelings within me. Relief that she lived. Sorrow that she was condemned to die. Guilt that I had inadvertently led the guards to her. And yet, beneath all of that, I remained calm. Because I was not alone anymore. I had Spider. And whatever time remained to any of us, at least I would spend it with someone who cared.

A few days after I heard that news about Maria, I came down with a very bad illness. I ached all over and ran a very high temperature. Spider nursed me and cared for me with the greatest tenderness I could possibly imagine, but the worried look in his eyes somehow seemed out of proportion to what were clearly only flu symptoms. Then a week or so later, just as we were getting our plan to send a message to Maria on track, I developed a bad rash on my back. But it cleared up after a few days, and I felt fine.

Then, just as I was convinced I was relatively healthy again, I awakened one night drenched in sweat. I did not think too much about it. I assumed it was probably a recurrence of the flu, and anyway, the nights were still very warm and I had been curled up against Spider because touching him made me feel safe and protected.

But the night sweats continued and on one fairly mild night I actually awakened Spider while I was walking around our cell trying to cool off.

"What is wrong?" he asked.

"Nothing really," I said. "I was just all hot and sweaty and I needed to feel the night air." I tried to make a joke, "I guess I just cannot cool down when I am around you." But Spider did not laugh. In fact he was very quiet. In fact he did not speak at all.

His silence was eerie. It made me nervous. I went over to his bed, sat down next to him in the darkness and put my hands on his face. I felt the moisture on his cheeks. I looked more closely and realized he had been crying.

"Hey, Spider," I said, "Why are you so upset? A little sweat never hurt anybody."

He still would not speak to me, and I found his behavior very strange.

I finally crawled back into bed, reached around his chest and rested my hand on his blue and gold tattoo. "What is wrong?" I asked.

"Oh, Sandro," he said, "you are sick, very sick, sicker than you can understand."

"Oh stop being such a worrier," I said. "Anyway, you are not a doctor. How do you know?"

"Because I am sick too," he said.

"Do not be silly," I said. "You are the most perfect physical specimen I have ever seen." But the way he said what he said had a certain finality about it that chilled me to the bone.

I held him closer, feeling the spider tattoo beneath my palm, feeling his heart beating against my chest. "What do you mean?" I whispered.

He was silent for a long moment. Then: "The night sweats. The rash. The fever that comes and goes. These are the signs, Sandro. The signs of the wasting sickness."

I knew what he meant. Everyone knew about the wasting sickness, the disease that had begun to appear in Central City over the past few years. A disease that destroyed the body's defenses, that left its victims prey to every infection, every illness. A disease with no cure. A disease that killed slowly, painfully, inevitably.

"But how?" I asked, though I already knew the answer.

"Strucker," Spider said softly. "He has it. He has had it for years. That is why they let him do what he wants. That is why they use him. He is already dead, Sandro. And now..." His voice broke. "And now so are we."

And on the 2,067th night of the drought, I did not sleep well at all.

Chapter Eighteen: Freedom

Freedom is meaningless. That does not mean everyone is not obsessed with the idea of being free. During those rare minutes when we are separated from all our daily responsibilities, when we are in a place apart from other people, when the wind is blowing in our face and we are heading toward the unknown, then a certain feeling rises up within us which we call freedom. And it is one of the most powerful feelings we ever experience.

But in fact, during the living of our lives, we are never free. And despite our most cherished myths and legends even the ancient ones were not really free. Our family is a prison; our faith, a prison; our city, state and nation: all prisons; our marriages and affairs are prisons; our work is a prison; our emotions and desires imprison us; our bodies, from the very moment we leave the womb, confine our spirits and restrain our ability to be free. So we must seek our true freedom within.

I, for example, never felt more free than I did during the short time Spider and I lived together in a cell that measured 6 meters by 10 meters deep in the bowels of the Central Penitentiary. The intensity of our love, the total commitment we made to securing each other's happiness, the routines of our confinement were all very liberating, and I was as satisfied as I could have possibly been during those days.

It was, in fact, my escape from the Central Penitentiary which caused me to lose my peace and freedom.

One morning we awoke to a terrible clamor. Everyone was

shouting and screaming, and we could hear explosions and blasts in the distance. In time the random and disorganized noise developed into a coherent chant which put my entire mind and body on full alert: "Brothers and Sisters know no fear. The Great Overthrow is here!"

Spider was, of course, happy and excited. "This is it," he said. "You will be rescued and assume your rightful place." He embraced me and kissed me, and despite my inner turmoil, it was comforting to see him so euphoric.

The chanting and explosions grew louder, and we were certain the penitentiary was being stormed by a popular uprising. Then pandemonium erupted inside the prison. There was smoke, the smell of sulfur, screaming, cries of agony and death, and the continued chanting which grew louder and louder. Finally different prisoners with keys ran to each cell and unlocked the doors while other prisoners ran about in an obvious state of confused delirium.

"Sandro," said Spider, "come. We must take you to the crowds who are calling for you. Come we must go."

As we wandered through the thick smoke and chaos, we realized the rebellion was already over and the prisoners were emptying the cell blocks and heading out into the yard. There were horribly mutilated bodies of prison guards missing heads and legs and arms, or with smashed limbs and torn stomachs with innards strewn about. There were also, occasionally, dead prisoners, presumably shot at the beginning of the uprising.

When we entered the yard, Spider insisted on lifting me up onto his massive shoulders and calling out, "Make way...make way...clear a path for The Chosen One." Usually the startled prisoners did step aside, and we were able to make our way to the front.

The prisoners had gathered at the main gate, and another crowd had amassed on the other side. Just as we reached the gate, the huge wrought iron doors came crashing down and the prisoners surged through the stone gateway to mingle with the protesters on the other side.

A man climbed on top of a flatbed wagon, and spoke to the chanting throngs through a device: "Behold, behold The Chosen One. Come, come and behold! Hear the words, and listen to the truth."

Spider tried to push forward, but this time his cries of "Make way...make way...clear a path for The Chosen One," fell on deaf ears. People laughed and pointed at me, mocking my crippled body, ridiculing my prison clothes and my deformities. Spider was angry and agitated, and I was almost thrown off his shoulders to the ground. "Relax," I told him, "relax, Spider. I think you will soon realize my denials were true."

"No," he said. "If there is another, he is an impostor, a false prophet."

At that very moment, the man with the device screamed, "Behold The Chosen One."

Everyone strained to see the person who then appeared on the wagon. It was Maria!

There she stood, so tall and regal. Her black hair had grown even longer and hung down all the way to her calves. Her skin glowed and her breasts were strong, full and round. Her voice was quite powerful and confident when she exhorted the crowd: "We must march on the city, citizens. We must gather up the dispossessed, and the resisting classes and march now! Victory will be ours. Follow me."

I thought she was wonderful as did most of the rest of the crowd. They moved in a vast human wave toward the city, gathering ever larger numbers as they swept across the countryside.

Spider was, however, disconsolate. "How can this be?" he asked. "The texts say nothing about a woman. They say nothing about a civil war. The Chosen One is a spiritual leader."

I tried to comfort him, but his sadness was truly profound. There was a small park about 200 meters past the burning penitentiary. I asked Spider to lower me to the ground, and I held his hand in mine while we walked toward the scrub trees and date palms.

When we reached the park, I sat down and propped my back against the trunk of a palm. I signaled to Spider that I wanted him to rest on the ground next to me. When he did, I said, "This is all for the best, Spider. I have tried to tell you I am not The Chosen One." He shook his head sadly. "I really am not," I said again, "but that does not mean I do not love you. Let me touch you once more, before this craziness pulls us apart."

I unbuttoned his shirt and licked the intricate strands of his web the way I had the very first time we were together. I licked his erect nipples, moved my tongue across his blue and golden tattoo, kissed his stomach and licked his navel, undid his pants and pulled out his beautiful member and drew on and licked and licked and drew on until we were both at the heights of frenzied ecstasy, and when he released I made him hard once more, and after that made him release yet one more time. Exhausted, I rested my head against his inner thigh and held his flesh against my chest.

I was almost asleep when I heard a vaguely familiar voice say, "Why are you not chasing the latest foolish Chosen like all the other fools?" Startled, I looked up.

What I saw was terrifying, the skeletal, ravaged face of an extremely thin man. His hair had fallen out in patches and there were reddish-purple lesions on his neck. His eyes had a demented look. When he coughed, he brought up blood which he discharged toward Spider and me. "Strucker?" I said. I had not seen him since that night in the chapel.

Spider leapt to his feet. Strucker tried to focus on both of us, but he staggered about and blinked a lot.

I did not really know what to say or what was going on, but Spider said, "So, we meet outside the prison, Strucker. This time I will have my revenge...for Sandro...and for myself."

Strucker again tried to focus on Spider and then me, but I, for one, saw no spark of recognition in his eyes. He coughed again and brought up more blood. When Spider moved toward him, he reached inside his pocket and pulled out a small, but wicked knife which he held in his shaking right hand. "Stay away from me," he screamed. "You, you...and you, stay away now, or I will, I will..."

"You will what?" said Spider.

For a moment Strucker seemed confused. Then he shook his head and blinked. "Why, I will...I will..."

"You will not do anything, will you?" said Spider as he confidently approached Strucker and reached out to grab the weapon from Strucker's hand.

But Spider's instincts were tragically mistaken. Strucker leapt forward and pierced the blue and gold on Spider's chest as Spider's forward momentum carried him into Strucker and the knife sunk deeper. Then Spider dropped to one knee.

I reached over, and picked up the cursed knife and walked toward Strucker. I fully intended to kill him, but Spider whispered, "No, The Chosen One does not kill!" Then with his last remaining strength Spider pulled himself upright and struck such a blow against Strucker's frail head he cracked Strucker's skull wide open and the monster was dead before he landed in a broken heap on the dusty ground.

Then Spider started to sway. I reached out to hold him up, but I was only able to cushion his fall. He laid there with his head in my arms as I held him close to me.

"I really do not mind dying now," he said, "with you next to me. I would not have wanted to end up like him."

"You would never be like him," I assured Spider, but he only closed his eyes and said, "You do not know. You are so innocent. All of us who are infected will all end up like that." Then he smiled and his eyes fluttered. He actually looked quite beautiful. The last thing he said to me was, "Sandro, I will embrace you on the other side, and you will again be my Chosen One."

Then, on the 2,569th Day of the Drought, Spider died.

I held him for a long time after his spirit left. I traced the spider tattoo with my fingers, feeling the smooth skin that would never breathe again. The blue and gold seemed to shimmer one last time in the afternoon light, the web catching the sun as if dew still clung to its strands. I kissed his forehead, his cheeks, his lips one final time. And I wept, not just for Spider, but for everything. For Mariann and Alexander, for Oswald and The Publisher, for the thousands dead in the square, for the beautiful acrobat family, for Dr. Pritowski's lost dreams, for my own shattered body and doomed future.

When the tears finally stopped, I began the work of burial. The ground was hard, baked by years of drought, and my mutilated hands made the digging difficult. But I worked slowly, methodically, until I had carved out a space deep enough. I laid Spider in the earth as gently as I could, positioning him so that his face caught the last rays of the setting sun. I did not want him to be in darkness immediately.

As I covered him with the dry earth, I spoke to him. I told him about the green plains where I was born, about the rains that used to fall, about the life we might have had together in a different world. I promised him that if I lived long enough, I would tell his story. That someone would know how beautiful he was, how kind, how he had saved me when no one else would.

I buried Spider right there in the park, marking his grave

with stones arranged in the pattern of a spider's web. I decided to let Strucker's body rot or become carrion for the wild animals, but when I finished marking Spider's grave and I was ready to leave the park, I could not leave Strucker's body like that. Instead I dragged a number of stones to where he had fallen and dropped them on him one by one until he was completely covered. It was not mercy. It was simply recognition that he too had been human once, before the disease and the violence had consumed him completely.

Then I looked toward the city and saw the massive clouds of black smoke. So I decided to walk in that direction, trailing behind Maria and her followers, toward the smoke and fires.

All along the way there was bloody evidence that the protesters had destroyed everything, and everyone who represented the Central Authorities. Bodies in uniform, or more accurately, parts of bodies in uniform, were scattered over the landscape. When I reached the outskirts of Central City, I could not help but notice that every police station, fire station, school, bank, and transmission tower was a shattered tangle of metal, building blocks and broken glass.

The city was unrecognizable. Places I had known, streets I had walked, buildings where I had worked were all transformed into ruins. I passed the storefront where the fortune teller had told fortunes, now a burned shell. I passed the warehouse district where I had hidden, now reduced to rubble. I passed the Queen's Revue, Oswald's sanctuary, its doors hanging open, its interior gutted by fire.

It was nighttime when I arrived at the Cathedral of The Living Truth. It was empty. Central Square was also deserted. I followed the crowd noises and ended up at the plaza in front of Central Headquarters.

There was an enormous fire in the middle of the plaza which was packed with tens of thousands of citizens milling about and causing each other all sorts of mischief or worse. Obviously law and order had completely broken down. The life of anyone even remotely suspected of collaborating with the Central Authorities was immediately forfeit. I personally witnessed six summary executions, one of a poor demented woman who did not understand anything that was happening to her and could not have been guilty of anything.

Suddenly every siren in the city sounded its screeching alarm. The doors of the Central Headquarters were thrown open and Maria appeared with her Citizen Guards and two other forlorn figures in tow. I recognized Tokorotan immediately, and the other looked like a much older version of the pictures we had all seen of the Supreme Leader.

Most of the activity in the plaza stopped as the crowd watched, in hushed anticipation, the performance unfolding in front of that building they had dreaded for so many years.

First a huge basin was brought from the building. Then Maria raised her arms and two Citizen Guards removed her clothes so she stood completely naked before the crowd. Then the guards sunk silver goblets into the basin and poured goblet after goblet of clear, clean water over Maria's body. The crowd, which had not seen such profligate use of water for many years, was stunned.

Then the Citizen Guards placed a large cauldron filled with bright burning red coals and handed Maria a gleaming silver dagger. They brought Tokorotan before her. She quickly and neatly sliced off his member and stones and ears. She held them up for the crowd to see before she tossed them on the coals. Then she ran the dagger through Tokorotan's heart, and her guards threw his body into the fire.

She repeated the process with the Supreme Leader, He whimpered and cowered and did not die so bravely. The Citizen Guards again washed her body with many, many goblets of water. Then they covered her with a white silk robe.

The crowd had watched the entire performance in completely stunned silence. When Maria raised her arms again and called to the crowd: "It is finished. The Great Overthrow has passed," they did not know what to do at first, then, as if on signal, everyone went completely insane.

I watched from the edge of the crowd, my mutilated body hidden in shadow, as Maria stood there bathed in firelight and water, the silver sword in her hand, fulfilling the prophecy in ways none of us had imagined. She was magnificent. She was terrible. She was The Chosen One, and I had merely been the fool who carried the message.

And yet, even as I watched her triumph, I felt a strange calm settle over me. Because I understood my true purpose. Not to lead, but to witness. Not to overthrow, but to endure. Not to bring the rain, but to survive long enough to see this moment.

I had carried the talisman, yes. I had suffered the tattoo, the torture, the violation, the disease. I had been broken and remade a dozen times. But all of it had been to bring me here, to this moment, to see Maria fulfill the prophecy that had been written long before either of us was born.

The Chosen One does not always know they are chosen. Sometimes they are chosen simply to bring the story forward so that others might know what happened on the Days of the Drought.

And so, on the 2,569th Night of the Drought, the rebellion succeeded and the Central Authorities were overthrown, but still, the rains did not come.

Chapter Nineteen: Death

Death is a silent stalker.

It would be helpful if our mortal sicknesses were always sig-naled by intense pain. But that is not the case. Few of us will die from childbirth, kidney stones, attacks of the internal or-gans, slipped discs, ruptured discs, broken limbs or torn finger-nails. Blows to the body, broken noses or ruptured eardrums are not usually fatal. Our bodies can handle enormous amounts of pain, and when the sensations are truly overwhelming, we simply overload and pass out.

No, death knows its prey quite well, and it prefers to go about its business without warning the host. Cancers spread through-out on secret pathways, bacteria settle into vital organs and viruses lie dormant in our nervous systems before we ever know of their arrival.

As for myself, although I had been battered and torn be-yond recognition during my adventures, I had come to be-lieve death would not overtake me unless it was by my own hand. However, that may have been because I could not see or hear or feel the inexorable changes inside me.

The doctors at the Citizens Institute of Health (once upon a time, the Central Institute of Health) heard my story, but they were mystified by it. They knew of no disease which dis-played the symptoms I described or followed the pathology I sketched for them. When I suggested they check the records from the Central Penitentiary, they told me there were no records, that everything had been destroyed in the uprising.

"But," I said, "if such an illness does exist, is it not important you know about it?"

"Well, yes of course," the doctors said.

"Absolutely," the administrators nodded.

"Without question," added the nurses.

But I never felt like they really believed me or showed much concern for the horror that was even then spreading throughout their city. They looked at me, this mutilated, scarred vagrant, and saw only another casualty of war seeking attention, perhaps seeking compensation for suffering. They did not see a messenger carrying news of a plague.

On my second visit to the Institute, there was a new doctor who was more interested in my story. She was young, tall. She had full breasts and wide hips and her white coat looked like it was meant for a woman half her size. Her high, wide forehead sloped down to the prettiest green eyes. She had a small nose, but a large mouth with thin lips and large white teeth. She wore six earrings in her left ear, two in her right, and one tiny diamond stud on the left side of her nose. She shaved her head because, as she later told me, "hair is dirty."

I was sitting in an examining room with my shirt off the first time she saw me. She gasped and turned her head away when she saw me naked, but she recovered quickly and smiled the biggest, most alluring smile I had seen since Spider died. "My name is Doctor Birelli," she said. "What in the name of all that is holy happened to you?"

I gave her a brief, cleaned version of my experiences with the Central Authorities before the Great Overthrow. Unlike others at the Institute she listened intently and asked questions. When I finished, she picked up my file and read through some pages. Occasionally she would look up from her reading and glance at me, then return to the file. Finally she said, "So, you think you have some unknown disease that is transferred by body contact?"

"No," I said, "I do not think that. I am certain of it." I then told her about Strucker and Spider. She winced a few times during the telling, but she generally handled her emotions with a great deal of control. "Well," she said, "I will be honest with you. The others have written in your file that you have a criminal mind, that you are untrustworthy, delusional, paranoid and probably psychotic. Any reaction?"

I smiled. "What do you think?" I asked.

"I do not know," she said. "Your story seems strange. There is no known disease with that wide a range of symptoms. Also, frankly we did not find any signs of disease when we examined you. Still..."

"Still what?" I asked.

She stood up, jammed her fists into her starched white coat pockets and paced around the small space available in the examining room. "There have been rumors, anecdotal stories, hushed discussions..." She stopped her pacing and looked into my eyes. "I have heard similar enough stories to be concerned. And," she said, "I do not happen to think you are insane."

"Thank you," I said.

"Do you think we could get a semen sample?" she asked.

"I can try," I said. "But I have not released for a long time."

Doctor Birelli went over to a small white cabinet and returned with a small glass container. "Please use this," she said.

She turned to leave the room, but I stopped her. "Would you stay?" I asked.

"Certainly not!" she said, but she did not walk out immediately. "Anyway, I thought..."

"Yes, I did love Spider, but..."

She frowned, and considered what she was going to do. Then she locked the door. "All right," she said, "what do you want from me?"

I pulled my member out of my pants and started to work it. She was immediately fascinated with the words tattooed on the shaft. "What do they say?" she asked as she reached down to touch my flesh. "No!" I shouted, "do not touch me!"

My panic stopped her. "Wait a minute," she said. She went back to the cabinet and returned with a pair of protective gloves. She stretched them, snapped the fingers and deftly pulled them over her hands. "Now," she said as she examined my member, "what is written there?"

"A woman's name and a date."

"Was she your lover?"

"She was my interrogator and my torturer."

"Oh my..." she said, but she was also a doctor and I doubt she failed to notice that when she released my member it did not return to its totally soft state.

"Please, stand with your back leaning against the wall," I asked her.

"Like this," she said as she stood with her hips and shoulders leaning to one side and her breasts thrust slightly forward.

"Like that," I said. "Now unbutton your coat."

"Do you want me to take it off?"

"No, just let it hang open."

She undid her coat and I was pleased to see she wore no covering beneath. My member was also pleased, and I have to say, in my opinion, the good doctor was also slightly excited.

"Now caress your left breast," I said.

She did.

"And pull on your nipple."

She did, and as she continued to pleasure herself her body moved and rolled against the wall. She aroused me to the point where I could easily work my member and feel the beginnings of release.

"Doctor," I pleaded, "Doctor, look at me; look into my eyes."

She was startled, I assumed because everyone found it difficult to look at my body.

"Do you need to have me cover myself?" I asked.

"No," she said. "No...I am all right. You are just so...so intense."

"And ugly."

"I do not find you ugly," she said.

"Put your other hand down your skirt on your sex," I said. She did, and then she moaned. After that she took the initiative, and actively pleasured herself while I worked my member faster and faster.

"Doctor," I whispered, "oh Doctor, Doctor, sweet Doctor, oh yes, yes, yes, Doctor, I remember now how...this...is...oh!...so...nice."

She climaxed at the same time I did, but still managed to remind me in a hoarse, forced whisper, "The container, Sandro, do...it...in...the...container...oh!...oh!...ohhhhhhhh!"

When we were finished, she opened the door and she was gone.

Three days later I was in her office. She was behind her desk studying my file again and looking at a series of laboratory reports. "I just do not know," she said. "We still do not see any sign of disease. Your sample is normal, healthy. Hmm... if it matters to you, your count is actually quite high."

"Are you suggesting I produce children?" I asked with a good deal of bitterness.

"I apologize," she said.

"Maybe I am disturbed," I said. "Maybe there is nothing wrong. It is just...just that Spider was so sure. He was absolutely convinced what happened to Strucker would be the end for us too."

"He was certain even though he appeared to be in perfect health?"

"Yes," I said. "Why?"

She did not answer me. Then she said, "Describe Strucker's symptoms again."

I told her about the lesions, the wasting, the dementia, the opportunistic infections that ravaged him. I told her how Spider had said we would all end up that way eventually. How the disease seemed to hide for years before revealing itself.

She was silent for a long time after I finished. Then she said, "What if it is not the sickness itself that kills? What if the sickness only opens the door for other things to enter?"

"I do not understand."

"Your body has defenders, Sandro. Tiny soldiers that fight off invaders. What if this disease slowly kills those soldiers? Then, years later, when they are all gone, any small illness could kill you because you have no defense left."

"That would explain why Strucker seemed fine at first," I said. "And why Spider showed no symptoms."

"Exactly." She stood up and began pacing again. "And it would explain why we cannot see anything obviously wrong with you now. The damage is happening invisibly, incrementally, over time."

She looked at me with something like awe. "Sandro, if you are right about this...if such a disease exists and is spreading through intimate contact...this could devastate our entire city. Everyone who survived the Great Overthrow could still die from this silent plague."

"Then you must warn them," I said.

"They will not listen to me. I am too junior, too female, too...inconvenient." She sat back down heavily. "But they might listen to you."

"They will not even listen to you, and you are a doctor. Why would they listen to me?"

"Because you are The Chosen One."

"I am not..."

"It does not matter if you are or not," she interrupted. "What matters is that people believe you are. That gives you a voice."

I shook my head. "Maria is The Chosen One. The people follow her, not me."

"Then go to Maria," Dr. Birelli said. "Make her understand. She has the power to act."

She mumbled to herself again, then said, "I need to take blood. I need to look deeper." She left the room and came back with a large-needled instrument. She walked over to where I was sitting and reached for my arm.

"No, Doctor," I said, "You are the doctor, but you still do not understand do you? Do not touch me!"

She pulled back, and quickly inhaled. "My god," she said, "of course you are right. If it is something hiding in the bloodstream..." She went for another pair of gloves and returned to take the blood sample.

As she drew the blood, I watched her face. She was concentrating intensely, but I could see the fear beneath. Fear that I was right. Fear that she was too late to stop it. Fear that she herself might already be infected through some accidental contact.

"How many others have you examined?" I asked.

"Three," she said quietly. "All with similar stories. All showing no obvious symptoms. One was a prison guard. One was a nurse who tended the dying. One was..." She paused. "One was a prostitute from the Red Zone who said a prisoner forced himself on her after the Great Overthrow."

"And you tested them?"

"I tested them all. I am waiting for results."

I did not hear from Dr. Birelli for a long time. Weeks passed. Then a month. Then two. I began to think perhaps I had been wrong, that Spider had been mistaken, that the disease was only in my imagination.

Then the Citizen Messengers found me in the homeless shelter where I was living and told me I should return to the Institute.

I did so the next day and found myself in a different office with a small tight-faced, severe little woman, Dr. Watt. Dr. Birelli sat on her left side. Birelli's eyes were red, her shoulders were slumped, her movements were slack and her hands un-animated. She would not look at me. She kept her head down.

The stern doctor spoke: "I have been authorized to inform you that there is absolutely nothing wrong with you, and that you may no longer take up the Central...uh, err, The Citizens Institute of Health's limited time and scarce resources for your obviously neurotic and possibly disturbed fantasies."

I glanced at Dr. Birelli. She shook her head ever so slightly. I looked at the older doctor. "That is it?" I asked.

She did not bother to respond. She stood. Dr. Birelli stood. They both left the room.

Later that night, the manager of the shelter came to my cot and told me I had a visitor. I went to the front and saw a tall young man in a dark brimmed hat. When we were on the street, I recognized it was actually Dr. Birelli dressed in men's clothes. "I had to see you," she said.

"Then I am sick."

Dr. Birelli took a deep breath and exhaled. "Well, actually, no. At least technically you are not. But..."

"But what, Dr. Birelli?"

She began to cry and it took her a few minutes to pull herself together. "I will oversimplify, Sandro, but essentially you have something that is very, very slowly destroying your body's defenses. The illness itself will not kill you, but, in time..." she started to cry again. Through the tears she said, "...in time you will get many, many diseases—other infections, growths, lung illnesses..."

"And they will kill me."

"Yes, they will kill you."

"Is there anything I can do?"

That question turned her tears to deep sighs of despair. "No, Sandro, there is nothing. We have nothing to give you. It may be a long, long time before we have anything."

"And," I said, "I will probably be dead by then."

"Maybe not," she said.

"But probably," I said.

She nodded.

"And the others you tested?"

Her face crumpled. "All positive. All of them. And when I tried to report it, they told me I was creating panic. They confiscated my research. They threatened me with dismissal if I spoke of it again."

"So they know," I said. "They know it exists and they are hiding it."

"Yes."

"So," I said, "What should I do?"

"Eat well, live well, avoid anything that can make you sick." She looked directly at me. "You told me once that you know the new Supreme Citizen."

"I knew her, yes, but I..."

"You could do all of us a great favor if you would try to see her."

"Why?"

"If not for yourself, then for me. I am so ashamed I do not have the courage to go against the authorities and alert the citizens. But the authorities are afraid of panic. The new government is shaky, and..."

"...But you think I could convince her."

She nodded.

"I doubt it," I said, "but I will try."

Dr. Birelli sighed. "Thank you. I know you have already given so much. Still...you may be the one chosen to..."

That word again. It made me shiver.

Suddenly she grabbed me, and because she was bigger and stronger, I could not stop her from kissing me. I was utterly horrified. "Why did you do that?" I screamed at her.

"Because I wanted to," she said, and then somewhat more carefully, "Actually my research indicates it is very hard to transmit without direct blood-to-blood, or blood-to-seed contact, Sandro. You can still touch people and they can touch you."

To make her point she kissed me again, tenderly and intensely.

And in that kiss, I felt something I had not felt since Spider died: hope. Not hope for my own survival. That ship had sailed. But hope that perhaps I could still do something meaningful with whatever time remained. Hope that Dr. Birelli's courage in defying the authorities might inspire my own. Hope that the story of the wasting sickness would not die with me in silence.

"Thank you," I whispered when she finally pulled away.

"For what?" she asked.

"For seeing me. For believing me. For not being afraid." I touched her shaved head gently. "For kissing me."

She smiled through her tears. "Will you really try to see Maria?"

"I will try," I said. "Though I do not know if she will see me. We have not spoken since the Great Overthrow. I was there in the plaza, but she did not know I was in the crowd."

"Tell her..." Dr. Birelli paused, thinking. "Tell her that The Chosen One has one final message to deliver."

I laughed bitterly. "I am not The Chosen One."

"Are you not?" she asked. "You survived torture, prison, violation, disease. You witnessed the Great Overthrow. You carry knowledge that could save thousands. You have been chosen for something, Sandro, whether you wanted it or not."

And on the 2,672nd night of the drought I began to learn to live with my own death and vowed to try and stop the deaths of others.

Chapter Twenty: Change

We all yearn for change both in ourselves and the world around us, especially when evil has taken control. If we are desperate enough, we will finally take enormous risks to bring about those changes we hope will lead to a better life.

But change has a way of disappointing us because it is virtually impossible to really get at the heart of the matter. So we strike at the surface and end up being satisfied with the ephemeral, convinced that at least we have done away with the worst of it. But after awhile it is hard for us to delude ourselves any longer.

Things changed in Central City. The old regime had been swept aside and a new regime was put in its place. That was all very well and good, except the new regime appeared to be evolving into a government suspiciously like the old one.

That feeling did not come to me only because of my experiences at the Citizens Institute. As news filtered out of Citizens Headquarters, I became ever more dismayed, and even more determined to try to stop the impending disaster.

It was true that instead of being called the Central Authority, the government was now the Citizens Authority. It was also true that my spirits soared when they unveiled the Monument to the Heroes of the Revolution, and I saw the names of Mariann and Alexander, Doebuck, Oswald Goodie, and the Reverend Armando Armandini permanently carved on a rich green marble obelisk sitting in the middle of Citizens Square.

However, not long after the dedication of the obelisk, I

learned The Publisher's First Assistant was the new Publisher of the old Authoritarian which had been renamed The Citizen. My irritation over that relatively minor announcement turned to outrage when they proclaimed that The Inquisitor was the new Director of Citizens Internal Affairs and Ashmir had been named the head of the Citizens Security Police.

So, I put in my formal request for a meeting with Maria, but I was told requests for an audience with the new Supreme Citizen were all being denied until the problem of the drought had been solved. Since I had nothing else to do, I spent my time and energy trying to organize a series of protests against the new appointments, but no one cared. Not one single person joined my lonely vigil outside of Citizens Headquarters.

Instead, I was roughed up by the Citizens Guards and told to leave the plaza. When I returned anyway, they beat me up again and confiscated my Citizens Stipend and my pass to the Citizens Shelter. So I built a shack out by the main highway near the cactus garden, under the eucalyptus trees, and I slept on the ground—hardly the prescription Dr. Birelli had suggested. But living there made it possible for me to get up each morning and harangue people as they entered the city, and to reprimand them for their complacency as they headed home each night.

I had one last burst of optimism when Eleanora was removed as Chief Justice of the Citizens Court, but that was quickly replaced with profound pessimism when I discovered the new Chief Justice was Prosecuting Attorney Rebecca. And that was not the worst of it.

I fell into a severe depression when it was reported that the Citizens Authorities were considering raising a huge expeditionary force that would cross the great dry river and sweep across the desert to wipe out the Shadowless Ones.

Each night the loudspeakers which had been strategically

placed around the city blared out reports of sabotage by the Shadowless Ones, and accusations that it was the Shadowless Ones who were diverting water and prolonging the drought. I do have to admit that although the reports were untrue, they had the effect of solidifying public support for the new government and Maria, our new Supreme Citizen. And so it went.

To tell the truth, my protests against The Citizens Campaign To Make The Desert Free were as ineffective as my actions to reverse those political appointments I had found so abhorrent. Worse, the authorities tore down my shack and forbade me to speak to people from the side of the highway.

As I grew more frantic and isolated from the events unfolding around me, my health deteriorated. I knew I had to talk to Maria quickly, before I died, but I could not figure out any way to get to her. Then, as often happens, pure chance, or perhaps fate, intervened.

I have to admit that for all their gentleness, once the Shadowless Ones were attacked, they did fight back with a resistance campaign that took advantage of their ability to go about unnoticed. At first they only hid explosives in places where they knew no one would be hurt. But when those actions proved ineffective, they launched a series of targeted killings against the Citizens government.

One day I was wandering through the city carrying my placard which said, "No More Fear! No More Sorrow! Bring Our Fighters Home and End The Drought!" when an official caravan sped by and nearly killed me. I fell backwards, and then, as I tried to pull myself out of the dust and filth onto my feet, a tremendous explosion threw me back onto the ground.

I looked in the direction that the caravan had been headed and I saw a number of wagons on fire. Bodies were strewn about. There was a lot of smoke.

As I stumbled forward to get a better look, Maria pulled herself through the broken window of one of the vehicles, stood for a moment in the middle of the road with a dazed look in her eyes and then crumbled in a heap on the pavement. I pushed forward, knelt next to her and cradled her head in my arms. She opened her eyes. "Maria," I said. "My Maria."

"Sandro?"

"Yes, Maria...It is me...It is me."

"Oh Sandro...what has happened to us?"

Suddenly from behind us, voices were screaming, "Get away from her! Get away! Now! Get away now!"

Maria pulled herself up and raised her hand. "Do not attack him! He must live. He must. He is a friend." Then she slumped against my shoulder. The Citizen Guards moved forward and we were surrounded. They lifted Maria, put her in another wagon and sped away. Then they hustled me off into a smaller wagon and drove me to Citizens Headquarters.

Once we reached the building, I was placed in a small room and left alone, although they did not lock my door when they left. A few hours later, guards opened the door and escorted me through the building until we approached two magnificent carved wooden doors with armed Citizens Guards in full dress uniform standing on each side. The doors opened and I was ushered inside.

Maria was standing with her back to me. "Leave us," she said to the others in the room; and when the various retainers withdrew, we were alone.

Maria turned around and faced me. She was still so beautiful, her face, her body, that smile. I was overwhelmed and realized anew how much I had missed her. She moved forward, we embraced each other. I felt her breasts press against my chest, and I buried my face in her hair.

We held on to each other for a long time. Then she stepped

back and looked at me. "Oh, Sandro," she said in a sad, shaking voice. She took a deep breath, trying to calm herself. Suddenly there were tears in the corners of her eyes as she looked at my ravaged face, my mutilated hands, my bent stance. "What happened? What did they do to you?"

"That is a long story," I said, "which I will tell you in time. But I must also ask, what have they done to you?"

"What do you mean? I am all right. I was not badly hurt in the accident."

"I do not mean today, Maria. I was talking about the new government, the war, the fact that the Great Overthrow came and went, and things have not changed."

"Sandro, you always were a dreamer, but even you can understand we must maintain stability until the drought ends. We cannot just overturn everything."

"Why not, Maria?"

Maria did not answer me.

"Maria, this war against the Shadowless Ones is wrong. I lived with them. They were not against you until you attacked them. And your appointments have been very unwise. I believe in your heart you know this."

Maria sat down and stared at me. Finally she spoke: "I thought you were dead." She was serious, thoughtful. "One of the reasons I have made these decisions is that I thought you were dead. Without The Chosen One, I was lost. What was I to do?"

"So, we are back to that?"

"Sandro, I am not The Chosen One. All of this is truly in your hands. Now that I know you are alive, I must remind you, you have the power...Will you accept your destiny? Will you end the drought?"

"If I can, will you end the war? Will you really set the people free?"

"Yes."

"Then what am I to do?"

"It is written that: The One Who Comes Before and The Chosen One must climb the mountain and stand among the clouds..."

"What then..."

"The Words do not say. I will go with you, then we will know." She walked over to the far side of the room, pulled back a curtain, opened the window, looked outside and then back to me. "There are clouds gathering on the horizon, Sandro. I believe it is time."

As she spoke, a slight breeze blew through the window, and I smelled the slightest hint of moisture.

I stood there, looking at Maria, and suddenly understood what the prophecy had always meant. Not that I would bring the rain through magic or divine intervention. But that I, broken, mutilated, diseased Sandro, was the price. My suffering, my degradation, my willingness to be destroyed and remade had been the necessary sacrifice. The rain would not come because I was powerful. The rain would come because I had given everything.

"And after?" I asked. "After the rain comes?"

"After, you must tell the people about the wasting sickness. You must warn them. That is your final task."

"And you will listen? You will act?"

"I promise you, Sandro. No more hiding the truth."

I nodded. "Then let us go."

Maria wrapped herself in a plain, hooded cloak and we left Citizens Headquarters through a series of secret passages that lead from the underground floors to a bunker and then out onto the street on the far northern edge of the city.

When we started our climb through the foothills, the light breeze we had felt in the city grew stronger as it shifted from the northern desert to the sea. The hint of moisture became a foggy wind. The air was damp and heavy. Large gray clouds continued to gather on the horizon.

Then the temperature dropped very quickly, and the chill raised goose bumps on my dry, cracked skin. Maria wrapped her cloak more tightly around her. The damp wind increased in intensity, and then it became a gale. I looked up and saw the clouds move inland. They bunched up against each other and turned the gray sky a thick, inky black. Then we heard low rumblings in the west, out toward the sea and saw the horizon illuminated by intense, bright light; but we were not deterred, and we kept climbing.

A few hours later, we left the foothills and started up the mountain itself. The thunder in the west had grown considerably louder. We heard a loud clap, then we heard tremendous rolling detonations which sounded like artillery exploding, and finally the sharp, startling noises that rattled my bones.

The thunder and lightning set the mountain dogs howling. With each sequence, the dark sky strobed and pulsated with jagged white light. The brown, thirsty scrub trees bent forward into the ever rising winds. I was forced to lean my weakened body at an extreme angle as we continued to climb, and eventually I needed Maria's help to hold me up. But we were able to keep going.

Then the temperature dropped even lower, and Maria wrapped her cloak around both of us to help shelter me. A particularly dramatic white flash ripped across the sky and a patch of chaparral not three meters off to our left erupted in flames. Smoke filled the air. Then another bolt landed off to our right. Then another crashed down behind us. My body filled with fear and my heart was beating so fast I was sure I would collapse. I was exhausted and frightened, but we both tried to move more quickly to avoid the gathering flames and so we struggled up the last kilometer to the top.

As we approached the summit, the first drops began to fall, huge globules of cold water raised little dust clouds in the hard dry dirt, "Splat...splat...splat." One drop landed on my forehead with such force it actually stung. Others sizzled on the smoking branches of the chaparral, "Tssst...ts-sst...splat... tssst..." Still we climbed.

Just as we reached the top and ran through the wind toward a large rock outcropping, the entire sky exploded white. I raised my head and in that extraordinary white light I saw huge torrents of water pouring out of the clouds and dancing on the surface of the ocean. I stood absolutely still, utterly transfixed as the storm moved inland.

Then Maria and I climbed atop a large flat rock that formed the highest part of the mountain. As we looked around at the fierce sky, the sea, the city, we were standing in a torrent.

Cold water ran down my face and my neck. I was shivering and shaking, freezing as Maria removed her cloak, stripped herself and then removed my clothes. Both of us raised our outstretched arms toward the sky, and we stood there naked while the water struck against our bare skin.

At that glorious moment my fear left me, and an enormous feeling of power swept over me. My member became erect. Maria took me in her hands and worked me. She worked and worked and worked as the water poured over us. Then she looked into my eyes when she felt my coming, and she grabbed my member with both of her hands, and she pointed it toward the dark black sky, and we watched my poisoned white fluids mix with the cold cleansing rains. Then we looked down and saw that my seed and the water created little rivers which joined a larger stream which fed a brook that washed down the mountain side across the land.

And on the 2,733rd and last Day of the Drought, the rains came.

I stood in the downpour, feeling the water wash over my scarred body, feeling it cleanse the dirt and blood and suffering of 2,733 days. I thought of everyone who had brought me to this moment. My fortune teller. Alexander teaching me to see. The Publisher sacrificing herself. Oswald's gentle courage. Reverend Armandini's faith. The acrobat family's beauty destroyed. Spider's love. Dr. Birelli's kiss. All of them had been part of this. All of them had been necessary.

Maria embraced me as the rain fell harder. "You did it, Sandro. You brought the rain."

"No," I said. "We all did. Every person who suffered. Every person who resisted. Every person who died. They brought the rain. I was merely the vessel."

Now the drought was over, but our work was not yet done.

Epilogue: Peace

It rained for fourteen days and fourteen nights. At first, there was panic in the streets. The babies and little children who had never felt rain or heard the thunder or seen lightning shrieked and tried to hide under their mothers' skirts. The forgotten smell of ozone and the downpour itself became the sources of rumors that the city was being poisoned.

But the rain eventually washed away the people's fear, and they rose up in open rebellion. Blood and water flowed in the streets, and the last vestiges of the old ways were removed.

When it was over, the sun came out for five straight days. Then it rained again. The hillsides turned bright, light green. The cacti were in bloom. The trees stood straight and tall. The air was fresh and clear. The sun was again yellow, and the sky was blue.

After the storms ended, Maria and I returned from the mountain to the city. As we made our way through the streets, crowds gathered around us, dancing and kissing the ground where we walked, throwing palm fronds at our feet, cheering and clapping and weeping from joy and happiness. By the time we reached Citizen Headquarters we led a procession of tens of thousands.

For a time after the Great Overthrow, the people believed Maria was The Chosen One. She led the crowd through the streets, she executed the tyrants with the prophesied silver blade and water of life. But when the rains came only after I stood naked on the mountain, when my seed mixed with the falling water and the drought ended on the 2,733rd Day, they understood. The One Who Comes Before is not The Chosen One. She prepared the way; I bore the cost. Maria brought revolution. I brought rain.

Maria and I were surprised to see the headquarters building was deserted, empty. The imposing metal doors had been ripped from their frames and lay shattered on the steps. Maria called for a torch, and when one was presented to her, she handed it to me. "Burn it," she said.

I slowly ascended the marble steps to the majestic entrance way and threw the burning torch into the building. The flames started slowly at first. Then they caught and spread, and the building burned throughout the night while the people danced and celebrated.

The next day Maria and I were approached by the NCC, the New Citizens Council. They asked us to rule the city. We agreed to consider their proposal, and when they left, Maria asked me what we should do.

"If we rule, we must rule in a new way," I said, "and I do not know what that would be."

"Do you want to rule?" she asked.

"No," I said. "I do not. But if we do not, who will?"

"I have been thinking," said Maria, "that perhaps we should pretend to rule..."

"Yes..."

"Pretend to rule, but actually do nothing."

I did not have to think too long about her proposal. "That would be truly wise," I said.

And so we have become the rulers by accepting their offer and pretending to rule. We have brought La Bruja in from her arroyo and installed her as our Chief Advisor. Whenever tough decisions are called for, Maria and I walk in our gardens while La Bruja does her magic. We accept, without question, her results. So far things have worked perfectly well, and the people are happy.

They certainly have nothing to fear from Maria or me. There will definitely be no House of Sandro. We have no desire to preserve our authority or maintain power so we can hand things over to those who come after us. What those who follow us do will be their decision, and we have both sworn not to concern ourselves about matters over which we have no control anyway.

Death no longer attracts or frightens me. During the first few months, I was weak from being on the mountain, from the sickness and the cold, stormy weather. Then, in the same way that the rains made the land grow and blossom, I too began to heal. My weakness has left me. I sleep without nightmares. The night sweats are gone. The rashes are gone. In truth I feel as healthy as I ever have.

And so I have decided I am strong enough to write down these words to help all of us remember and perhaps someday, before we end, to understand what has happened to us.

But those will not be easy things to understand. For the moment, I am satisfied to walk around these beautiful gardens and appreciate peace's healing ways.

Yesterday, I was sitting under the new growth on one of the old, magnificent trees that survived the evil, dry years. In its struggle to survive, the tree had let one large bent and twisted branch die and fall to the ground. Now there is a large, rounded swelling protruding from the trunk where the branch once hung. I ran my fingers over the surface of the swelling and felt its texture, the smooth and the rough places, the curve of the arch.

In the middle of the growth there is a dark, circular area, an areola which presses out from the larger swelling. As I brushed the tips of my fingers across that growth, I felt a soft, sticky liquid emerging from a small opening in the center. I licked and smelled my fingers and noted that the sap was thick and abundant and intoxicating.

Under the tree, near the trunk, scattered among the roots, the rains had stimulated the spores of a bed of mushrooms. Their smooth, brown parabolic crowns sat on top of long, curved shafts. I laid down next to the bed and inhaled the musky fungi. I closed my eyes and placed my lips on the head of the largest growth and thought of Spider.

Then, when I rose from the ground to leave the old tree, I noticed a flash of bright magenta beneath my left sandal. I shifted upwards at the very last second, just before I would have crushed it. My movement sent me sprawling so I crawled over to the splash of color and discovered a single, fragile flower.

I knelt before the bloom on my hands and knees and peered down into the flower's delicate interior. The fused petals were arranged in a perfect opening, the magenta around the outer edges gave way to pure white except for a thin streak of yellow which divided each of the three petals into equal segments. The petals themselves were smooth yet firm. I leaned over, lowered my face to the flower and very carefully let the tip of my tongue lick the insides.

The gateways to life are very, very precious.

And so I have decided if I am to be known as The Chosen One, then my message is the ebb and flow of the life force itself, and that union with that force is all we will ever know of freedom, freedom to feel our living abd freedom for our minds to soar beyond the limits of our struggles.

And I have resolved that whatever else happens, on the day I die, when all of these memories pass before my eyes for one last time, I will smile and say, despite all I have been through, "It has truly been a wonderful life."

And it has...

Rain

Book Two
Der Drei Elemente

Guillermo Bosch

Sandro, the legendary Chosen One who, in Rain, the first book in this series, brought water to save a dying land, has retreated into his palace, believing his work complete. But a new tyrant, the golden-haired Alejandro Alejandrisha, rises to power using corruption and evil magic.

Fire, a very adult fairytale explores timeless questions: Can love truly overcome tyranny? Is forced salvation still genocide? What if evolution could be chosen rather than imposed? With its unique blend of mythic storytelling, complex moral philosophy, and visceral imagery, Fire will appeal to readers of literary speculative fiction that doesn't shy away from difficult questions about power, transformation, sexuality and what it means to be human, or post-human.

Prologue

This is the second tale of my story. In the first, I told of drought and rain, of how I became the Chosen One, of how Maria and I brought water back to our dying land. That story ended with abundance.

This story begins when abundance failed us.

Ten years have passed since the rains returned on the 2,733rd Day of the Drought. Ten years since Maria and I withdrew from power, determined to rule by not ruling, leaving La Bruja's wisdom to guide what we refused to control. The old virus, the wasting sickness that spread during the final Days of the Drought, has been contained through bitter knowledge and Dr. Birelli's warnings. La Bruja's spells hold my own infection in abeyance, neither cured nor killing. But peace and prosperity, like drought, can also be a curse.

So, as we begin, the land had transformed utterly. Each morning brings pewter skies that turn black with bloated, billowing clouds. Winds rise from the west, and fresh showers soak the welcoming ground. During the afternoons, the sun blazes through the depleted dome and coaxes even more growth from the fertile, soggy soil.

Tumbling rivers course through once brown arroyos. Waves of grain roll down steep mountainsides. Jade forests sprout where previously no tree rooted.

And with that fertility, great wealth has descended upon Usa Visral, the name we have given to Central City once we finally rid ourselves of the old regime. Enormous machines with long curved necks and sharp teeth sliced shimmering leaves, crunch nuts from tall thin palms, pluck beans from short curling vines, and dump the abundant harvest into massive wagons. These are the same wagons that, in earlier and darker times, carried citizens to their death and now carry the lifeblood of the people.

But with this wealth comes a terrible forgetting.

Money has captured the hearts of our people. Money collected, invested, spent with abandon. Hard times are banished from collective memory, and with those lost memories something essential has been lost: the storytellers are silent. Fortune tellers are ignored. Temples and worship houses are empty. Children work alongside their parents because each shiny coin helps families secure a larger shelter or a sleek, speedy transport.

So it is on this 3737th Day of the New Rains when I realize that solving one curse often brings another.

I seldom leave our palace to mingle with the people. I remain the Chosen One, a title given to me after the Great Overthrow and earned through suffering I will not recount here, but that title had little meaning in a world where everyone lives a chosen life. What does it mean to be chosen when all are chosen?

But the screw turns and the curse arrived.

On one sultry evening as my life consort, Maria, and I strolled through the palace gardens, we stopped to admire the latest exotic plant imported from jungles in the Distant Lowlands. Our Violet Trumpet was a beauty: thick ropy tentacles, enormous seductive blossoms, prominent black velvet stamen. The plant had wrapped itself around the trunk of a slender date palm in what seemed an embrace but was, in truth, a slow strangulation.

I should have read that omen.

We heard the explosion first, a thundering crack, then a rumble outside the palace grounds. Almost immediately, thirty meters of our sturdy limestone wall crumbled, and floods of brown foaming water swept into our garden. The date palm's shallow roots were ripped from the earth. The beautiful Violet Trumpet was swept away along with the tree, and Maria and I found ourselves trapped against a small corner of the remaining wall.

The water was two meters high and rising. The current was too strong for swimming, but Maria, as she had done before, as she would do again, found a way. She managed a foothold between the remaining old stones, pushed with her powerful legs, and with the fingers of her right hand found another tiny crevice in which she was barely able to establish a hold.

Meanwhile, I slipped beneath the water.

This is what I remember: I could not see. I could not hold my breath. My chest was burning. Darkness swept across my brain. I lost all will to resist and felt myself rapidly losing consciousness, drifting off into the swift current toward oblivion.

Then there was Maria's hand, a vice grip on my left wrist. Slowly, so very slowly, I felt myself being pulled upward and back, though the raging water fought to claim me. Then my head broke through into the air, and I was spitting and coughing phlegm and foul-smelling filth.

Maria pulled me out of the water onto the broken stones. Then she hauled me over her shoulder, and we inched along the top of the rocks until we reached the corner where the wall connected to the palace. From there we climbed through an open window into an empty storeroom and stumbled up the stairs into our bedroom, where we collapsed onto our silver and purple canopy bed.

When I awakened, Maria was curled next to me, her light brown arms cradling my head against her soft, naked breasts.

"The gateways to life are precious," she said, smiling.

"What?"

"That is what you wrote in the first telling. Do you not remember?"

"Yes...I do...but..."

Maria's voice turned soft, playful. "I am a gateway to life, Sandro. You may enter."

She reached down and held my flaccid cock in her hand.

I was astonished. Truly, utterly astonished. We had not had sex since that night when we held each other while thunder and lightning crashed over the mountains, when our coupling brought the rain that ended the drought. Even then, we had released my seed into the air to fertilize the gathering clouds, not inside her body.

"No, Maria, no...the old virus..."

"But the virus is not inside me, Sandro. I can be a gateway to life, a new life. We can make a new life together."

She continued to fondle and stroke my cock, and it grew despite my desperate attempts to smother arousal.

"Maria! You could be sick. If we make a child, the child could be..."

She interrupted. "We will speak to La Bruja. She will cast a spell."

"La Bruja has..."

"Great powers, Sandro."

"She does, but even she has not been able to cure me."

"She could not cure you. It is too late for a cure. But she was able to hold the virus in abeyance. You are not sick. Not yet. Not now."

She continued to touch me, and I was getting larger. My shallow breathing turned to panting. I stared into Maria's eyes. My hands sought her breasts. I could not stop kneading them, could not stop needing them, could not stop my fingers from stretching her nipples, could not stop my mouth from taking each extended nipple between my lips, my tongue from circling around each tip, my lips from sucking.

As I grew even larger, Maria gasped. I grabbed her around her waist and pulled her back toward me. I lowered my head between her legs, my tongue finding her smoothness, her wetness. My hands held her thighs. Her back arched off the bed. Her breathing quickened.

Then she pushed me onto my back and straddled me, just as she had done the first time she rescued me, so very long ago. She held my organ with both hands and gently inserted me into her passage. She exhaled deeply, then her hips began a rhythmic rotation, her breasts gently rocking in time with her movements.

I was lost.

I reached up and cupped her breasts. My eyes bored into her eyes, and hers into mine, our connection from the early days, from the first telling. Slowly, rotation evolved into swaying and bucking. As she reared back and pushed hard on top of me, I raised my buttocks off the bed. My seed rose inside me with a slight burning sensation. I tried to withdraw, but Maria's legs were locked about my waist, and I could not escape as I came inside her. She threw her head back. Her curls whipped from side to side. There was an urgent sound deep in her throat, and then she fell forward onto my chest.

"Thank you," she murmured into my ear. "Thank you."

"Thank you?"

"For making our baby."

"Oh, Maria, you cannot say that..."

"Shhh," she said. "I can say that. We will go to see La Bruja. Everything will be alright. I promise you. Everything will be alright."

But she was wrong.

Nothing would ever be alright again. Not in the way we then understood "alright." The world we knew was ending, and a new world was being conceived, not just in Maria's womb but in the very fabric of those times.

This is that story. The story of how a new world was born. The story of how the Chosen One dissolved so that his son could transform everything.

The story of Fire...

Rain

Guillermo Bosch